PERRYN'S BLOOD THUNDERED IN HIS EARS. HE READ
the prophecy again and again. His whoop of joy echoed from
the stone walls, and the scroll rolled shut as he danced wildly
around his room.

The dance ended abruptly as he tripped over the edge of
an old chest and fell to his knees. He pushed his spectacles
back into place, unraveled the scroll with fingers that trembled, and read it again.

ALSO BY HILARI BELL

A Knight and Rogue Novel: *The Last Knight*

The Prophecy

The Wizard Test

The Goblin Wood

A Matter of Profit

HILARI BELL

THE PROPHECY

An Imprint of HarperCollins*Publishers*

Eos is an imprint of HarperCollins Publishers.

The Prophecy
Copyright © 2006 by Hilari Bell

Library of Congress Cataloging-in-Publication Data
Bell, Hilari.
    The prophecy / Hilari Bell. — 1st ed.
        p.   cm.
    Summary: Guided by the words of a prophecy, Prince
Perryndon, who loves books more than swords, sets out
to slay the black dragon that is destroying his kingdom.
    ISBN 978-0-06-059945-4
    [1. Princes—Fiction. 2. Bards and bardism—Fiction.
3. Unicorns—Fiction. 4. Dragons—Fiction. 5. Magic—
Fiction.] I. Title.
PZ7.B38894Pro 2006
[Fic]—dc22   2005018150

Typography by Karin Paprocki
❖
First Eos paperback edition, 2007

For Anna Maria—the friend whose insightful advice made this book, finally, work.

This is the story, as told by the bards,
of Prince Perryndon, who set out to
slay the black dragon guided by
the words of a prophecy.

In all the great libraries of the land,
Prince Perryndon studied the lore and
history of dragon slaying.

PERRYN WAS ON HIS WAY TO THE LIBRARY TOWER when the master of arms' shadow fell across his path. He jumped, and Cedric's hand closed around his shoulder.

"It's time for your sword lesson, Prince Perryndon. Had you forgotten?"

"But . . ." Perryn's thoughts spun. *Cedric hasn't come after me for months. Father. . . .*

"Is my father home?"

Sunlight flooded through the arched windows, but it brought no more warmth to the master of arms' face than it did to the gray floor and walls of the castle's upper hall. Cedric's eyelids dropped, concealing his gaze.

"I don't think it's my place to answer that, Your Highness. Would you please come with me?" He started toward the side stair that led down to the practice yard.

Perryn braced his feet, resisting, and the scarred hand tightened on his shoulder. He tried not to flinch. Cedric's body was long and lean, hiding his strength. It fooled people, until he proved his strength on them.

"I'll go," said Perryn, "if you answer my question. Is my fath—"

"You'll go anyway." Cedric shoved him in the direction of the stairs.

Perryn staggered, but regained his balance before he fell. Whenever Cedric caught him alone, the respectful facade slipped.

Cedric hovered over him as they walked down the stairs, giving Perryn no chance to escape. His tanned face revealed nothing, but Cedric's face never showed anything unless he wanted it to.

The king must have returned from riding the borders. Cedric never hunted him down unless his father was home— why put on a show unless you had an audience? Usually Perryn could elude the master of arms, but his father had been gone for so long that he had become careless.

In the small armory that adjoined the practice yard, Cedric watched him fumble with the buckles on his armor. The

anger and fear rushing through Perryn's veins made his fingers shake.

"Would you like me to help you, Prince Perryndon?"

"No."

When he was finished, Perryn removed his spectacles and set them carefully on a high shelf. They fit too awkwardly under the helmet Cedric made him wear. He had cracked a lens once and spent a week groping through a blurred world before the town glazier could grind him a new one—and then his father had complained about the expense. After that Perryn had chosen to fight without them, though their absence made it impossible for him to see the small, warning twitches of Cedric's sword.

Perryn put on his helmet, pushed up the visor, reached for his shield, and slid his arm through the straps. He lifted his sword. It was almost too heavy for him with just one hand, but he managed.

Perryn clanked around Cedric and into the practice yard. Fuzzy lumps of color were all he could see of the guardsmen who stood around its edges. He thought he saw more of them than usual. Perryn hoped he appeared dignified, but he knew it was unlikely. Once he'd overheard a guardsman say that he looked like a puppet whose joints were too loose.

That was mostly because his armor was too big. When the metalsmith made it, just after Perryn turned thirteen, he'd said that the prince would grow into it. That was over a year ago, and the stiff metal joints still hit his limbs in the wrong places. It was excellent armor, well crafted, fit for a prince ... a prince who was three inches taller than Perryn.

Cedric stepped up in front of him. The arms master was giving instructions, but he spoke so softly that Perryn could barely hear him. It did more harm than good anyway, when he listened to Cedric's instructions, for Cedric never did what he said he would. He'd tell Perryn to set his guard for high blows, then swing for his knees. Or promise a set of slow, practice forms, and then attack at full combat speed.

The master of arms wore no armor or helmet, carrying only a shield and a blunt-edged practice sword. Perryn's sword was sharp, showing everyone that Cedric knew the prince couldn't hit him. Perryn usually didn't care, secretly grateful for the protection of his clumsy armor. But today his father was home. Probably watching. He squinted up at the windows surrounding the practice yard, but all he could see were hazy shadows.

A crushing blow struck his breastplate. Perryn stumbled back, tripped, and found himself sitting on the ground. The

visor clanged down, obscuring what little remained of his vision. He heard the guardsmen snickering, and his face grew warm inside the concealing helmet.

"Always keep your attention on your opponent, Prince Perryndon." Cedric's voice was serious and respectful—playing to his audience. "In battle, a man will take any advantage."

A teacher shouldn't. But Perryn didn't say it aloud. He knew that his father would agree with the master of arms.

Perryn shoved back his visor, hauled himself to his feet, and picked up his sword. His blade was sharp. Cedric wore no armor. *And my father is watching.*

After teaching Perryn for four years, Cedric hardly bothered to guard himself. Why should he, since Perryn never swung at him?

Cedric started to stalk him, and Perryn backed away. His stomach was tight and quivering—fear of the blows, fear of humiliation, which could hurt even worse. But Algrimin the tactician had written that catching your enemy off guard was half of winning. If he was careful to give no warning, maybe he could hit Cedric. Just once. *With my father watching.*

Cedric rushed toward him.

Perryn tried to leap back, but the heavy armor defeated him. He got his shield up, but he was off balance, and the blow knocked him sprawling.

The snickers turned to open laughter.

Perryn barely noticed. His shield arm hurt, but his sword arm was fine, and for some reason the shaking in his belly was subsiding. He picked up his weapon and stood again, staggering slightly.

Cedric saw it. He began circling Perryn, but his pretense of wariness was just that—he was performing now, for the laughing guardsmen and the watching king. His attention wasn't on his opponent.

Perryn jumped forward and swung his sword low, at the unprotected legs beneath the shield.

Cedric leaped away, but for once he was too slow! Perryn felt the tip of his sword catch something. Then Cedric's shield slammed into him. Perryn flew back, struck a wall, and slid down it, half stunned.

Rough hands jerked the helmet from his ringing head. "He's all right," Cedric announced, without bothering to ask him.

Cedric's legs were right in front of his face. Perryn thought there was a cut in his leggings, but he couldn't see

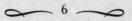

any blood. What was that beneath the cloth? He squinted, bringing his vision into focus.

Padding, thick enough to deflect anything but a strong, well-aimed blow.

Tears rose in Perryn's eyes. He blinked them down, dragged himself to his feet, and stumbled back to the armory to find his spectacles.

ONE OF THE MENSERVANTS WAS WAITING FOR Perryn when he returned to his room. He had drawn the prince a hot bath.

It would have been churlish to refuse. Perryn had never understood why the castle servants treated him with respect, when the guardsmen all despised him. Perhaps it was because they'd been the ones who cared for him, after his mother's death. But they'd cared for his father, too, in his furious, shattered grief. However, his father didn't seem to remember that time—he still didn't know the names of half of the menservants who escorted him, stumbling up the stairs.

But all the servants, from the steward, Halprin, to Dis, the scullery boy, had been on Perryn's side ever since he could remember. And he returned their care with gratitude. So, he took a bath, which eased some of his bruises, and ate the meal they brought, although he didn't really want that either. It wasn't until he reached the library tower that he was able to put the afternoon's humiliation behind him.

The library tower was *his* place. No one else ever climbed the long flights, past all those rooms of dusty paper. No one had ever organized it either, each king's clerks shoving chests of papers and stacks of books into any vacant spot that took their fancy. Perryn had turned the room at the top of the stairs into a study, cleaning it himself, furnishing it with ink and pens and his favorite books. His most prized possession, a turning globe of the stars that had belonged to his mother, stood by the windows.

Perryn had been only four when she died, but he still remembered . . . not her face, but the feel of her: soft, warm arms around him, as he sat on a velvet-covered lap and watched her hands turning the globe; the scent of lavender. He also remembered a father who had returned from the summer campaigns laughing with joy at seeing his family again, tossing his small son high into the air before he settled into a solid hug. Perryn wasn't sure how accurate his memories were; he sometimes wondered if his liking for books had come from her.

Though he loved reading for its own sake—history, natural science, the old bardic lays, any book he could get his hands on—Perryn spent most of his free time methodically sorting through room after room of books, records, and scrolls, searching for any reference to dragon slaying.

The room he was working in now held mostly documents from the reign of the sixth king, a time when dragons were nothing but a misty legend from the northern mountains. Perryn opened the chest without excitement and read for several hours. Only four scrolls remained, and his grimy fingers left smudges on the paper he unrolled.

> *The dragonslayer must be a true bard, one who sees and sings the truths that are hidden in men's hearts.*
>
> *He must have with him a unicorn, a creature of such purity that its tears can cleanse the blood of dragon's wrath.*
>
> *And he must slay it with the Sword of Samhain, whose steel, tempered with courage, can withstand the dragon's flame.*
>
> *With perfect truth, purity, and courage, even a dragon can be slain.*

This I have seen in a vision come to pass, and
this I prophesy.
  To this I set my hand,
  Mardon the Magus

Perryn's blood thundered in his ears. He read the prophecy again and again. His whoop of joy echoed from the stone walls, and the scroll rolled shut as he danced wildly around the room.

The dance ended abruptly as he tripped over the edge of an old chest and fell to his knees. He pushed his spectacles back into place, unraveled the scroll with fingers that trembled, and read it again.

For five years Perryn had been searching the dusty tower for those words, for any words that would give instructions, even a hint, of how a dragon might be slain. Now he held a prophecy made by the greatest magus and seer that had ever lived. Mardon, who had guided the fifth king to ally Idris with the six southern kingdoms. Mardon, who had foretold the invasion of the Norse barbarians centuries before the first attack. In that age no dragon had even been seen in Idris, so this must be a true prophecy! He had to show it to his father!

Tucking the scroll in his belt, Perryn hurried down the

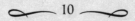

spiral stairs, past the rooms full of history books, land deeds, tax records, and scrolls of poetry.

Bards were fewer now, but surely a true bard could be found. There had been one in the castle only last week. Perryn had been in bed with a cold and hadn't seen him, but he'd heard something about trouble with Steward Halprin.

In fact, contrary to the castle gossip, Perryn was seldom ill. He was thin and small for his age, with pale hair and skin, but it was only because Cedric complained so often about Perryn missing his sword practice that many people thought he was weak and sickly.

The tower steps ended in the long hall. Perryn rushed down it, careful not to brush the faded tapestries with his dirty clothes.

A unicorn would be harder to find, although people claimed to have seen them in many of the histories Perryn had read. One book, *Animal Footprints* by Ebron the Hunter, had shown drawings of unicorn tracks. Searching stubbornly for dragons, Perryn had generally skipped over these references. Now he would have to go back and find them again.

He grabbed the rail at the top of the great stair and let his own momentum spin him onto the steps, which he hurtled down, two at a time.

Had the Sword of Samhain been buried with the twenty-eighth king? No, it was King Albion, the twenty-seventh! Perryn didn't remember reading about the tomb's location, but that didn't matter. The details of any king's burial were a matter of historical record.

Perryn crossed the great hall in a rush. A bored guard stood before the double doors to the dining hall, a sure sign that his father was still there.

"Wait, Your Highness," said the guard urgently, as Perryn reached for the door handle. "You don't want to go in there. The king is . . . I mean, King Rovan doesn't like to be disturbed after dinner."

"It's all right. I have good news."

But Perryn hesitated for an instant. Everyone knew that the king drank deeply in the long nights of the early spring. Or, at least, it once had been only in the spring. Now . . . Perryn wiped his grimy hands on his tunic and slipped quietly through the door.

His father sprawled in the chair at the head of the long, empty table. The dirty dishes left by the army officers who dined with him had been cleared away—only the bottles, and the cup in his father's hand, remained. His moody gaze lifted at the sound of the door closing, and Perryn breathed a sigh of relief. He could tell from his father's eyes that he wasn't too drunk to understand.

"Don't stand there cowering. What do you want, boy?"

Perryn flinched, but he drew a deep breath and went to the head of the table where he pulled out a chair and sat next to the king. "I have news, Father. Wonderful news!"

"You've learned how to kill something bigger than a spider? You haven't been at sword practice for months. You think I don't know that, but I do. I asked Cedric. He says you hide from him when it's time for your lessons."

Perryn's gaze fell. It had been years, not months, since he had started avoiding sword practice—hiding from the master of arms, who never looked very hard. "That isn't important. Not compared to this." He held up the scroll.

"You can't use a scroll to skewer a Norseman through the guts when he comes after your life and your kingdom. Someday I'll be gone and you'll be the one fighting them, boy. Then, by the gods, you'll wish you'd learned to use a sword when you had the chance."

"But we've held the Norsemen at our borders for more than forty generations. Surely..."

"Yes, that we have. Oh, surely. But that was before the dragon came, sapping our strength raid by raid, village by village. For more than fifty years. You know what I'm doing now? Trying to recruit troops for the summer's campaign. Going from town to town looking for landless men to train for men at arms. Used to be they'd flock to the gates of Idris Castle. Now we have to beg them to stay and fight instead of running south. They run anyway. Scared of the Norsemen, they are. Scared of the dragon. Scared of everything."

"Father, I'm talking about the dragon. I've found a prophecy!"

The king drained his cup. "Prophecies are cow flop, Perryn." He poured more wine.

"But it tells us how to slay a dragon! We need a bard, a true bard...."

The king snorted. "You mean a tune plucker like that scoundrel I kicked out last week after we caught him sneaking into the wine cellar? What for? To sing little dragon-wagon a lullaby? To sing the death dirges for the slain?" The king took a long drink.

"A *true* bard, Father." Perryn drew a steadying breath and pressed on. "And a unicorn, to heal the fever. And the swor—"

"A unicorn! Where in this gods-forsaken land do you think you're going to find a unicorn? And I've seen that fever you're talking about. 'The dragon's wrath.' It burns

14

through a man's blood, killing him in hours. No dainty uni-corn is going to stop that hot death. A kinder death than a cold one, though. Maybe they're right, that the dragon can only be fought with magic. Maybe we were doomed from the start."

Perryn felt his heart sink at the mention of his mother's death. Remembering what had happened to his wife always set the king on the path to oblivion.

"But a prophecy *is* a kind of magic." Perryn held hard to his courage. "Why should the dragon be the only magical creature left in the land? We can find a unicorn! And the Sword of Samhain!"

The king's laugh made Perryn wince. "A *sword*? Against that iron-skinned monster? Our sharpest blades barely nicked it. Our arrows bounced off as if it were made of gran-ite, and it crushed us like beetles in our armor. And the cannon . . ." The king's face twisted with grief. "When we fired the cannon, it took to the air and soared above us . . . as the snow fell and your mother died. A sword against that? You read too many books, boy."

"But Father, if this is a way to kill the dragon—"

"Kill the dragon? I wouldn't be surprised if you ended up *bargaining* with the dragon, as the Norsemen do."

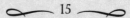

"I would never do that. How can you—"

"Then you'd better learn to use a sword, boy, or you'll wind up in their first group of sacrifices . . . once we've been conquered."

"If we fulfill the prophecy and kill the dragon, Idris might become strong enough that we couldn't be conquered! If—"

"If that dragon could be slain, I'd have done it. When I'm gone, the Norse will sweep through Idris like a scythe and all the seven kingdoms will be open to them. Idris is the shield, and if it falls, it will become an open gate."

"But Father—"

"Stop bleating at me. There'll be no more books for you. And I'll teach you swordplay myself. You'll be too busy for prophecies then. You may never be much of a man, still less a king, but I'll make what I can of you."

The bitterness on the king's face echoed in Perryn's heart, and he rose to his feet. "If you feel that way, then why did you bring me back when I was nine? You could have let me go."

"I almost did. University. What a dainty thing to run away to. You should have been dreaming of adventure, of great battles. You're fourteen now. You should be almost

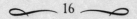

ready to be knighted. I'm the forty-fourth warrior-king of Idris, and you'll be the forty-fifth. You, with your books and your specs, like an old granny. But you're the only heir I've got. So you'll be the forty-fifth warrior-king and not some worthless scholar."

"But . . ." Tears rose in Perryn's eyes and he forced them down. His father despised tears. "How can I make you listen?"

"By *making* me," said the king. "Come on. Give it a try."

He grabbed Perryn's collar and rose unsteadily to his feet.

"Guard!" He dragged his son over to the door, hauling him upright when he staggered. "Guard!" The door swung open. "Take . . . oh, it's you. Get him out of here, Cedric. He's pestering me. Found some cow-flop prophecy about dragon slaying."

He flung Perryn into Cedric's grasp and closed the door.

But the prince's enemies
learned of the prophecy and sought
to slay him.

2

CEDRIC MAINTAINED HIS BRUISING HOLD ON Perryn's arm as he hauled him to his room, though Perryn knew better than to struggle. The master of arms pushed him inside and slammed the door behind him.

Perryn sat on his bed and curled his arms around his knees. Five years of work, wasted. He'd hoped for so long that if he found a way to slay the dragon, his father would recognize the value of his studies. Maybe even allow him to go south, to study in one of the universities. But now....

Defending Idris' borders was his father's duty, but killing the dragon was his obsession—and even that hadn't been enough to overcome his prejudice against scholars! How could he be so blind? This prophecy gave them a chance to destroy the dragon. At least, in theory.

That was the problem. His father wasn't open to theory; he would only accept proof. If Perryn could just prove it....

He looked for the scroll, but it wasn't in his belt. Had Cedric taken it as he'd dragged Perryn along? Could he simply have dropped it? Perryn had a good memory for anything he read, but he'd still like to get it back.

He went to the door and pressed his ear against it. When the master of arms left, he could return to the library tower. In his excitement, he hadn't even finished searching the chest. Demothar the alchemist said that you must never allow enthusiasm to impede critical thought. There might be more information.

Cedric was still in the hall, giving someone orders. A hammer? A bolt? The servant's voice lifted in protest. He had no authority to put a bolt on the prince's door.

Perryn raised a fist to pound on the wood, then let it fall. He might persuade the servant to refuse, but it would only get the man into trouble. Cedric was not above taking revenge on a servant when the king was gone, and his father usually left Cedric in charge. The summer campaign against the Norse would start as soon as the snow melted in the northern passes—probably just a few weeks from now.

Perryn went back to his bed, listening to the hammer

blows that turned his room into a prison. Why would Cedric do this? Perryn wasn't going anywhere. He had nowhere else to go.

Installing the bolt didn't take long. After they left, Perryn tried the door—it didn't budge. Had the king ordered this? Why? He'd proved the futility of running away five years ago—and the humiliation of being hauled back by the guards had smarted even more than his father's thrashing.

The servants would bring Perryn's meals, but what about his studies? He always left the books and scrolls in the library tower, ever since the day one of the maids had thrown out several piles of "dirty old papers." As a result his room was perfectly proper for a prince—and bare and boring. It was in his study that Perryn really lived. Could the servants bring him the chest from the library tower? Probably not. Even if he could describe it clearly enough, Cedric or his father might hear of it. Either one of them was capable of ordering the contents burned. It was too risky. Besides, there was another way that might work.

Perryn went to the trunk at the foot of his bed and dug through his summer clothes until he found the Mirror of Idris. He lifted it carefully; it was startlingly heavy for

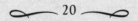

something that was only a hand span across, and the glass between the twisting silver serpents was very old.

No one knew why the gods had departed the world, but they had, and now no man was born with the gift of wizardry. The magical creatures the gods had created survived and bred, but the magic made by men was different. Some people, Perryn knew, didn't believe that magic existed anymore, but the Prince of Idris knew better.

Once, the kings of Idris had used this mirror to observe events from one end of the continent to the other. When it was new and strong it could speak with its own mind-voice, show the past, and even the near future. But it was wizard-made magic, not god-made, and like all things made by man, it weakened with time.

As generation succeeded generation, the mirror stopped revealing the future and the distant past. It spoke seldom. Then never. It could see no farther than Idris' borders, but it still showed what it could to Idris' kings—and to their heirs.

Perryn's father had once used the mirror to keep an eye on his army's clashes with the Norsemen on the border. It was beginning to function erratically, even then, but it was still useful most of the time. It had lain in a place of honor on the king's council table.

For more than a month before Perryn's mother died, it had showed nothing but sheets of roaring, tumbling snow.

Everyone knew that the mirror showed the kings of Idris what they needed to know, which wasn't always what they'd asked for. But when the vision never seemed to change, Perryn's father decided that the mirror had finally failed and ignored it.

When he returned from the dragon's valley, without his wife, he told the servants to take the mirror away, that he never wanted to set eyes on it again.

Perryn had found it in the library tower. He'd tried to use the mirror, but it seemed that the effort of foretelling his mother's death had drained all but the dregs of its power. Or maybe the problem was that Perryn was only a king's heir, and an unworthy one, according to his father. Whatever the reason, the mirror had never showed Perryn a scene farther away than the fields around the castle, and it often functioned wildly, displaying a stabled mule when he asked it where his father was.

He seldom troubled it anymore, but this was too important not to try.

"Mirror of Idris, I am Perryndon, Prince of Idris, and I seek your aid."

The mirror worked best if he spoke to it slowly and clearly.

A swirl of darkness washed through the glass, then it stopped reflecting Perryn's face and settled into darkness. Perryn felt a prickle of excitement. The mirror was listening.

"Mirror, I have found a prophecy about slaying a dragon, made by Mardon the Magus. Can you show me anything else written about that prophecy, or about dragon slaying?"

Light flickered in the depths of the glass. Perryn tried not to hope too much. The last time he'd asked for documents about dragon slaying, he'd gotten an inventory of castle tapestries from the reign of Narin, the fourteenth king. Perhaps the mirror thought he'd needed that, but if he did, Perryn still didn't know why.

The mirror flickered again, and a picture appeared. Perryn fought down a surge of disappointment. This was a document, shown from a distance, but it was being written as he watched, and the mirror had never shown Perryn anything more than a few days past, much less the future. Probably some court paperwork.

"Thank you for trying, but . . . wait." The hand that held the pen was Cedric's. Perryn recognized the long, big-knuckled fingers and crisscrossing scars. But Cedric was illiterate! How could he possibly . . . ?

"Mirror, show me what he's writing more closely."

The image grew larger.

My Chieftain,

Something unexpected has happened and I must kill the boy.

I have kept him from learning anything about arms, and the soldiers will never follow him. The king drinks heavily and will probably not survive to grow old, even if you cannot take him in battle. Since all looked so promising, I saw no harm in letting the boy waste time in the library.

But he has found something. There is a prophecy, made by some past magus, of a dragon being slain by a bard using the Sword of Samhain. Those here do not respect magic as they should. We, who have lived in the shadow of dragons from the earliest times, know better. If all goes as we plan, their ignorance will be their downfall.

This sword was lost long ago, but magic

often finds a way to raise itself. The boy is too
weak willed to do anything on his own, but if he
convinces his father to go looking for that
sword, the dragon might be killed.

   If Idris were prosperous and well manned,
it would be almost impossible to conquer—
it is proving hard enough, even with the dragon
eating away their strength from within.

   So I will kill the boy. It can be made to look
like an accident.

   Keep pushing the borders, my chieftain.
Sooner or later the rotted tree will fall.

Cerdic of the Red Bear

The hands in the mirror concealed the letter under a loose floorboard and left it there. Perryn sat, staring at the board for a long time before he told the mirror to let the picture go. His hands were cold with fear, but for once they weren't shaking. Indeed, he felt as if his whole body was frozen in place. At least his mind still worked.

He could go to his father. The letter was proof.

But by now the king would be too drunk to understand, much less to act. And Perryn didn't have the letter—only

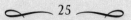

his word for what he'd seen. His word against Cedric's.

No, he couldn't tell his father.

Still, he had to tell someone! A spy, a Norseman, in the king's confidence, privy to all his plans. No wonder the war was going so badly! But who could he tell? The servants had no authority over the guardsmen, and Cedric—*Cerdic?*—did. Was there anyone who could help him? He'd had no friend in the castle besides the servants since old Ovis, his tutor, had died. And even if there was someone he might have appealed to, his door was bolted shut.

An accident. It could happen tonight. Right now! Perryn sprang to his feet and then sank back. No. Probably not till everyone was asleep. He had time to think.

He gazed out the window into the cold spring night. The clouds blew across the face of the waning moon, creating shadows that swept across the landscape. A perfect night to slip past the guards—if he dared.

. . . too weak willed to do anything on his own.

He could go south to one of the great universities. Become a scholar, as he had always wanted. He would be safe there. Unless the barbarians really could conquer the seven kingdoms, if Idris fell. With a traitor in their midst? *When* Idris fell.

This I have seen in a vision come to pass, and this I prophesy.

Perryn's heart pounded. The wandering bard had been gone for only four or five days. He couldn't be too hard to find, and even if he wasn't a true bard he might know of others who were. As for the unicorn...

Alirian the teacher once wrote that discovering facts and piecing them into truth is a scholar's job. A true bard, a unicorn, and the Sword of Samhain. If Perryn could piece these elements together, if he could actually make the prophecy come true, his father might respect him for what he was, instead of trying to make him into something he never could be.

Might. But if he did nothing, then nothing would change. Ever.

... too weak willed ... Curse Cedric, and all his plots and opinions!

Perryn turned from the window and began making plans.

*Prince Perryndon set forth in search
of a true bard, wise and courageous.
Weaker bards had fled south, to safer kingdoms,
so only the greatest of bards remained in the land.*

3

PERRYN TIED THE LAST TWO STRIPS OF BLANKET together and tugged at the knot. It should hold. The thick wool was very strong. He slung his satchel over his shoulder, then he went to the window and lowered his improvised rope quietly down the wall. The soft scrape of cloth against stone sounded loud to him, but the wind made enough noise to mask it—and hopefully louder sounds as well—from the guards who patrolled the parapet above him.

He climbed onto the windowsill and sat, looking at the ground. He wasn't afraid of heights exactly, but it was a long way down. Perryn wrapped both hands around the blanket strip and slid off the windowsill.

As the cloth jerked tight under his weight, the knuckles of his right hand slammed against the wall, and Perryn gritted his teeth. His shoulder swung painfully into the stone. He was heavier than he'd expected, and the satchel added even more weight. The thick blanket strip was hard to hang on to. He didn't dare look down, and not only from fear of the height. If his glasses fell and broke, it would stop him right here. He should have thought to take them off before starting down! Some scholar he was.

The brisk breeze turned him against the wall, making him sweat with nervousness. Perryn climbed slowly down his improvised rope. He stopped looking up to see how far he had come. He never looked down. Then his groping feet slipped off the end of the blanket, causing him to gasp, even as his hands clamped tight around the rope.

The ground was farther than he'd hoped. He tried to slide his hands down, but without the bracing grip of his feet, he could barely hold on. He pushed himself away from the wall and let go.

The drop was even farther than it looked—the earth slammed into his feet, then his knees, with bruising force. Perryn sat up and rubbed his elbow. Then he rose to his knees and pushed his spectacles back into place. The palms of his hands smarted and stung. His knuckles were bruised and his arms ached. But he was down!

A grin spread across his face, then he remembered—the mirror! He snatched up his satchel and scrambled to the base of the wall, fumbling the buckle open, groping hastily through the folds of his warmest cloak. His fingertips found the silver curve, then skimmed over the cool glass—not broken. Not even cracked. Perryn barely stifled his exclamation of relief in time.

He'd almost chosen to leave the heavy mirror behind, but it had served the kings of Idris faithfully for centuries and it had certainly proved useful tonight. With luck it might show Perryn documents from his library when he needed them, or allow him to watch his father and Cedric. If he could see what measures they took to find him, he could avoid them, and if he could avoid them long enough.... His father might worry now, but that couldn't be helped. He would have to earn his father's belief, his trust, before he accused Cedric. And if the king worried, if he feared for Perryn's safety, it might remind him that he had once loved his son, as well as the wife he had lost.

Yes, this was the right thing to do.

He repacked the satchel, which also contained the bread and cheese he'd been offered for dinner and the handful of coppers he was given each week to reward the servants. With careful management, it should be enough.

His father called the library a worthless waste of paper, brushing aside Perryn's muttered arguments, but Perryn needed more information about the habits of unicorns and the location of the king's tomb. Still, even if the mirror couldn't help him, a true bard should know both those things.

Perryn waited for a cloud to hide the moon so he could run for the nearest clump of bushes, though he wasn't really worried about the guards. Idris Castle was far from the Norse border. The guards looked at the sky, not down into the bushes, and in the darkness they listened for the sound of dragon wings.

Clouds covered the moon, and Perryn darted off. In a few minutes he would reach the trees. He thought of his mare, now dozing in her stall, but there was no way he could get a horse out of the stables without being caught. He would walk. Peasants walked from place to place all the time—surely a prince could do the same. There was a shortcut through the forest to the nearby village of Bramlin. If the bard had passed through there, someone might know where he went next.

Perryn was on his way.

"Excuse me?"

The tavern maid bustled past without even a glance at the dusty stable lad. The tavern in Williten was full of customers, all demanding service, but still ... Prince Perryndon would have commanded instant attention at any inn. But he wasn't Prince Perryndon now, Perryn reminded himself, and that was a good thing.

"Excuse me, but I'd ..." She was gone. Perryn sighed and slumped back against the wall, remembering the long day behind him.

The bard had gone through Bramlin, a sleepy stable boy had remembered for free and been persuaded for a copper to swap clothing and forget that he had ever seen his prince. Once he assumed his disguise, Perryn felt safer asking other people about the bard, but no one in Bramlin seemed to know where he had gone next. The two nearest towns were Durnst and Fair Meadows. With no idea what the bard's intentions were, Perryn had guessed Durnst. It took him several hours to walk there, only to find that the bard hadn't gone to Durnst after all. Then it took several more hours to retrace his steps and take the crossroad to Fair Meadows.

The name had suited the village two years ago, before

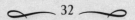

the dragon had struck. Perryn had watched the flames of the attack from his tower, sick with sympathy—and with guilt for doing nothing, even though he knew there was nothing he could do. He remembered his father's helpless rage.

The lean, grim-faced villagers of Fair Meadows got four coppers from his purse before they revealed that the bard had gone east from there. At least they hadn't recognized Perryn. These men would have turned him over to anyone who offered them a coin. Remaining unnoticed was the only way for Perryn to elude his father. Fortunately, Fair Meadows lay north of the castle. His father would assume he'd fled south, as he had before. It might be weeks before these men were questioned, and hopefully they wouldn't even remember a curious peasant boy. The sun had been setting when Perryn trudged into Williten and located the crowded inn.

He heard the tavern maid's quick, light tread approaching once more.

"Excu—" Perryn found himself looking at her back again as she whisked away. He reached into his purse and pulled out a copper piece. The tavern maid appeared before him as if by magic.

"Can I get you something, young sir?"

"Just some information. I need to know if a bard passed through here a few days ago, and where he went from here."

"Oh, I can tell you that." The copper vanished into her pocket. "He did good business in the taproom for several nights, the saucy scoundrel. He played that old harp of his to a treat. Made everybody merry. That's why Pa was so peeved when I . . ." Her eyes slipped down, and she blushed. "We weren't doing anything, really. But Pa said . . . well, he asked Lysander to move on. Anything else?"

"No," said Perryn, slightly stunned. "Wait! I mean, yes. Do you know where he went?"

"To Drindle." The girl gestured to the west. "At least, that's what he said. But frankly, he's not the type a girl would do well to believe, if you know what I mean."

"Wait," said Perryn again, as she started to move off. "Is there somewhere I can sleep tonight, for a copper or two? I don't have much money."

"Two coppers for the stables, there's straw in the loft, water in the well; three coppers for breakfast, pay in advance," the girl recited crisply.

Perryn fished out two more coppers, which disappeared as quickly as the first. "Thank—" She was gone.

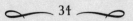

Perryn grinned and tucked his purse back in his belt. It was lighter than it had been this morning, but some things were going right—no one would think to search for him in a stable loft. He picked up his satchel and went out, unaware of the man who watched him go.

THE STRAW SCRATCHED THROUGH HIS CLOAK. Perryn turned and turned again. Exhausted as he was, he'd expected to fall asleep quickly, despite the fact that the straw pile in the stable loft wasn't nearly as comfortable as his own bed. At least it was quiet. The horses in the stalls below made little noise beyond the occasional thump of a restless hoof. And as for the smell, well, he liked the scent of horses and dusty leather. So he should be sound asleep right now, but instead, he lay thinking.

Was his father worrying about him? And what about Cedric? What would he do, now that Perryn had fled? Could he damage Idris irreversibly, if Perryn took too long on his quest? The letter to his chieftain had sounded like the Norsemen were planning for the long term, making slow, sure moves. Still, it might be too soon to try the mirror again, but maybe not. The mirror was notoriously erratic.

After a few moments of groping in the dark, Perryn settled back with the mirror on his lap. Even when he put on his spectacles, all he could see in the dimness was a faint gleam of light off the glass.

"Mirror of Idris," he said softly. "I am Perryndon, Prince of Idris, and I seek your aid. Show me..."

My father's reaction to my flight. But wasn't it more important to find out about Cedric's plans?

"Show me the reaction to my flight." He would let the mirror determine what he needed to see!

The dim reflection of his own face was a pale blur in the mirror's surface. Perryn held his breath. A moment passed. Another. Disappointment welled in his heart. It was too soon. The mirror was drained—

Suddenly the reflection glimmered, swirled, and began to glow. Perryn leaned forward, staring at the picture that formed there. A road. No, a fork in the road, with the main road continuing on and a smaller track branching off into some hills. Thick bushes surrounded the lesser branch, and although Perryn couldn't see into their shadows—it was night there as well—it was clear there were no people present.

Perryn sighed. It was too soon to try again. He should let

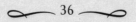

the mirror rebuild its strength.

"Thank you," Perryn murmured as the vision faded. He knew he should put the mirror back into his satchel, but his own weariness swamped him and he set it aside, thrusting it into the straw near his boots. He would repack everything in the morning.

SEVERAL HOURS LATER PERRYN SHIFTED REST-lessly, not quite asleep, but not awake either. He heard a rustling in the straw beside him, followed by a tug at his belt, and brushed at it sleepily. Another tug. What was it? A rat?!

Perryn jerked upright, flailing at the straw beside him. A strong hand grabbed his collar and thrust his face into the fabric of his cloak. He couldn't breathe! He struggled help-lessly. Cedric? No, please! A hard yank at his belt—his purse! Bright spots were forming in the darkness behind his eyes. The hand on his collar yanked him up, and he gasped for air. The world went black.

HIS JAW HURT. WHY WERE THERE WOODEN RAFTERS above his bed instead of curtains? Perryn groped for his spectacles but he couldn't find them. He reached up and touched his jaw. A swelling bruise. It hurt. Not Cedric, a

thief. His purse was gone. He was sleeping in a stable, and his purse was gone. But what about . . . the mirror!

It took several minutes of searching through the straw near his boots to find it, but at least the thief hadn't noticed it. Losing his money was bad enough. The tears that rose in his eyes were tears of relief, Perryn told himself firmly.

"I will not give up," he said to the empty loft. "I will not go back, and I will not turn south."

Running south at the first sign of trouble would *prove* that Perryn was as worthless as his father claimed, and tears wouldn't help him get his money back. Perhaps the tavern keeper could. Perryn groped his way to the ladder.

The tavern keeper offered many consoling words, and so did his wife and daughter. They found Perryn's spectacles in the loft—undamaged, thank goodness—but they didn't agree to replace the money he had lost, or even supply him with breakfast. They did offer to send a groom to fetch the mayor, but Perryn refused. Machidius wrote that it was the duty of all men to assist in the apprehension of thieves, but the mayor might recognize him. He would certainly remember the incident when Perryn's father came in search of his missing son.

The thief had gone through his satchel and evidently

decided that Perryn's bread and cheese weren't worth stealing, but his food was nearly gone anyway by the time Perryn tramped wearily into the small village of Drindle. It was mid-afternoon, and the tavern there had only one customer.

The tapster's gaze moved slowly from Perryn's dirty boots, past his scrapped knuckles, to his bruised jaw.

"Money first," he said.

"I haven't any money," Perryn admitted.

"Then get out."

Perryn gritted his teeth. "Please, all I need is some information. I'm looking for a bard. I think his name is Lysander."

"Oh, him. He left town this morning. He had enough money to stay the night, but after that we asked him to leave. This is a hard-working village—we don't encourage vagrants." The tapster's gaze was very direct.

"All right," said Perryn wearily. "Just tell me where he went."

"How should I know?"

Perryn's shoulders slumped in defeat.

"If I were a bard, I'd go to Dunstable," said the customer. "It's the only town in the area of any size and there's a market day tomorrow. A big crowd with lots to spend. Your bard will be there, or I miss my guess. I'm going myself, as soon as the smith fixes my wagon wheel."

Perryn turned to study the man. He had big shoulders and a friendly face. "You're a farmer?"

"That's right. I'm going into Dunstable to pick up some seed. Planting time is almost here, and you've got to put something into the ground if you want something back."

The tapster snorted. "If the dragon doesn't come along some cold autumn night and burn your harvest to ashes."

The farmer gave him a sympathetic glance. "He's from Fair Meadows," he told Perryn quietly, and Perryn nodded in sudden understanding. "My wagon will be empty on the way out. I can give you a ride, if you want it."

PERRYN FELL ASLEEP IN THE JOLTING WAGON AND didn't wake until they rolled onto Dunstable's noisy cobblestones.

"It's getting lively already," the farmer noted as Perryn scrambled onto the seat beside him. They were part of a long, slow-moving line of carts heading toward the market square.

As Perryn rubbed the sleep from his eyes and adjusted his spectacles, he saw that the town teemed with people: farmers, housewives, craftsmen, and merchants. He'd never been

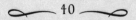

in a town this large—the village that served Idris Castle was smaller, and when he'd run away before he hadn't gotten very far. The clamor of voices echoing off the cobbled streets and stone walls was disconcerting, though Perryn tried not to show it. The Prince of Idris shouldn't gawk like a country bumpkin.

Then the shutters of an inn flew open, and a man sailed out onto the road. The crashes and thuds of a brawl reached them through the open window. The man rolled to his feet and ran back into the tavern. Shouts for the town guard rose from people on the street. Perryn realized he was staring, but he couldn't seem to stop.

The flow of carts carried them closer to the brawl. The town guard was coming. Perryn swallowed, trying not to look as nervous as he felt.

"Don't worry," said the farmer cheerfully. "The guard will take care of it."

Two burly guardsmen pushed through the crowd and into the tavern. The crashes and thuds grew louder, then began to dwindle.

"You see," said the farmer. "Just like I said."

Two guards emerged, dragging a slender young man with torn clothes and tangled, light-brown hair. His nose was bleeding onto his brightly embroidered tunic, but he still struggled in the guards' grip.

"My harp!" His voice was clear as a tenor bell. "You dragon-blasted fools, my harp's in there! I'm not going anywhere without it."

"You're going with us, like it or not," the shorter of the two guards panted.

"Either you let me get my harp, or I shall report your uncooperative conduct to the mayor himself," announced the bard. He'd stopped fighting and stood straight, looking almost dignified in spite of his disheveled clothes and hair.

The taller guard snorted. "What makes you think he'd listen to you?"

"Because I know his daughter, Hyacinthe," said the bard. "I saw her just last night." The tall guard became very still. "She was with *you*. Of course, she didn't call herself Hyacinthe then. What name was she using? Alyce? No, Anise, that was it. Tell me, does the mayor know . . . ?"

The tall guard turned and went back into the tavern. A moment later he emerged carrying a gracefully curved but battered harp, which he shoved into the bard's waiting hands. The three of them went off through the crowd together.

The farmer was laughing. "Your bard?"

"I suppose he must be," said Perryn ruefully, climbing down from the cart. "I'd better follow them. I thank you, sir, for all you've done."

"My pleasure," said the farmer. "And don't worry about following them. You'll be able to find your bard in the town lockup anytime in the next month, or I miss my guess. Take care, lad."

Perryn bowed and set off to find the jail.

But the bard was held in durance, by evil men,
and Prince Perryndon was forced to labor
mightily to free him.

"SO THEN I LOOKED IN HIS BAGS AND—"

"—swindling me, the toad, right from—"

"Silence!" roared the justice, for the fourth time.

"But it—"

"I—"

"Excuse me," said Perryn, trying to wiggle through the crowd in the public hall. "Excuse me, please." No one budged.

"Bailiff, throw them both in a cell!"

Silence fell around the justice's chair.

"Ah, that's better," said the justice. "Let me see if I've managed to understand all this. You, sir, are a tavern keeper, who employed the bard Lysander to entertain your customers."

Perryn saw a three-inch gap between two broad backs and lunged for it. "Excuse me."

"Employed, hah," the bard responded. "A pallet on the floor, scraps from the tables, and permission, *permission!* to keep the coins people offered, while I brought in crowds of—"

"I took you in, fed you, housed you, and you repaid me with theft, you—"

"Bailiff!"

"Excuse me." Perryn struggled onward. The crowd was getting thicker, and the noise level was rising again.

"And you, Lysander, feeling that the tavern keeper was underpaying you, decided to increase your wages without his knowledge?"

"It wasn't theft," said the bard. "This miserly rogue offered me all I could eat, if I honored his filthy hovel with my playing."

"Filthy! Hovel!"

"Silence!"

"Excuse me. Excuse me. Excuse me."

"I've heard enough," the justice declared. "Tavern keeper, we will return the food the bard was taking. Next time, be more careful of the character of those you employ. And as for you, master bard, there can be no doubt that you planned to steal from the tavern keeper."

Perryn wedged himself between two more bodies and squirmed. He couldn't wait while the bard served a long sentence. His father would surely find him, and all his plans would come to nothing. Disastrous for him, and maybe for Idris, too.

"You have also caused a public brawl and disturbed the king's peace," the justice continued. "Therefore, I sentence you to ninety days in lockup. If you want to take any of our jail food with you when you go, feel free."

"But you can't do that!" Perryn burst through the crowd at last. "I need him."

The sudden silence was even more absolute than the hush produced by the justice's previous threat. Everyone stared at him. Perryn belatedly remembered that interrupting the proceedings of a court was illegal. The impulse to run seized him. *Weak willed.* He forced himself to meet the justice's gaze firmly.

"I beg your pardon?" the justice said.

"The boy is my brother," said the bard quickly. "Dependent on my care. Just look at the state he's in! He'll starve if I'm in jail. It was for him I took the food."

"Is that true, lad?" asked the justice.

"Ah, well, no," said Perryn.

"You ungrateful cur!" exclaimed the bard. "After all the years I've fed you, clothed you—"

"Silence!"

"But I do need him," said Perryn. "If I have to wait here ninety days...well, it will be too late. Please, sir, is there any way you could reduce his sentence?"

"I could impose a fine instead." The justice scratched his chin. "It should be ... hmm. Ninety coppers. Do you have ninety coppers, lad?"

"No."

"No money at all?" The justice eyed his patched, dusty clothing, and Perryn blushed.

"I was robbed yesterday," he explained.

The justice's brows rose. "I've heard nothing of this. Did you make a complaint?"

"No," said Perryn. "That is...it was in another town, and I was traveling on. I didn't want to cause trouble."

Contempt flickered over the bailiff's face, and Perryn realized that he sounded as weak as Cedric claimed. Anger rose instead of tears. Who cared what some local jail guard thought of him!

"Isn't there any other way?" he asked the justice desperately.

"Hmm."

Perryn, struggling not to look pathetic, changed his mind. He needed their sympathy, even their pity. He let his desperation, his embarrassment sweep over him. Tears brimmed, running hot over his cheeks. Miraculously, the bard remained silent.

"This is most irregular," the justice complained. "I really don't see..."

"Please," said Perryn. "It's very important."

"Humph. We can't have you wandering the streets without a copper for ninety days, that's for certain." The justice rubbed his chin thoughtfully. "I'll make you a deal. You say you want this man. Out behind the jail is a big pile of wood. We've gotten low on kindling over the winter. A woodcutter could chop it in two or three days, but he'd charge us a gold piece for the job. That's a bit more than ninety coppers, but it's going to take you longer. You can sleep in the jail kitchen, we'll feed you, and you can have your bard as soon as the wood is chopped. Until then, he's a prisoner. Good enough?"

Perryn wiped his face hastily. "Most fair, sir, and I accept with gratitude. But..."

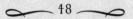 48

"But?"

"But I'm not sure I want him. I mean, I'm not sure that it's him I want. Sir, may I speak to this man alone for a moment? Please?"

"Oh, if you must." The justice gestured toward an empty corner behind him. "Bailiff, watch them."

"That's remarkable," said the bard before Perryn could speak. "I never saw anybody who could cry on cue like that. Even traveling players have to use an onion. Is it hard to learn?"

"Are you a true bard?" Perryn demanded. "Really a true bard?"

And if he wasn't, what could Perryn do? How many bards were left in Idris? Could he even find another?

"I'm a bard," said Lysander. "For what it's worth, which these days is practically nothing. I don't know what you want, but whatever it is, you're unlikely to get it from me. All I have is my harp, and that isn't for sale."

"Can you see and sing the truths that are hidden in men's hearts?"

Perryn held his breath.

The bard's face went still.

"Yes. I can."

"Can you prove it?"

The bard laughed. "How?"

Perryn thought. "I'll chop the wood," he said finally. "I've never used an ax before, so it'll take a while. While I work you'll write a song. A song that—"

"Reveals the truths and so on and so on. I understand. What happens if you don't like the song?"

"Then I leave the last ten logs in the woodpile untouched, and you rot in jail for ninety days."

Lysander studied him. "You're serious, aren't you? What do you want? Really?"

"There's . . . a task I want you to perform. If I get you out of jail quickly, will you do it?"

"How quickly?"

"As quick as I can. I don't want to be here any longer than I have to, but I don't know how long it will take."

The bard shrugged. "It shouldn't take more than a week. And whatever you want, it's got to be better than wasting the summer in lockup. All right, if you get me out, I'll perform your task."

"Do you swear that?"

"I give you my oath as a bard," said Lysander grandly. "Let's go tell the justice, shall we?"

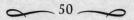

THE AX WAS LONGER THAN PERRYN'S LEG AND
the most awkward tool he'd ever encountered. He'd seen
woodsmen at work around the palace, so he knew the basic
theory; but theory, as he was discovering, was very different
from practice.

"Try hitting the wood with the edge of the blade, not the
flat," suggested Lysander from the barred window.

Perryn glared at him. He was already regretting that the
bard's cell overlooked the woodpile. "Don't you have something else to do? If you haven't written a song by the time I
reach the last ten logs..."

He swung the ax again.

"At this rate I'll have a hundred days to write it. Maybe if
you gripped the handle a little higher?"

"The wood turned as I hit it." There had been nothing
about chopping wood in any book he'd ever read. Perryn
removed his spectacles and wiped the sweat out of his
eyes. The blisters on his palms stung. He'd be able to concentrate better if he weren't so worried about what
Cedric was up to. At least there were no other prisoners
to observe his unprincely clumsiness. "I don't need
advice from a musician—and a lazy musician at that.

Don't you have a song to write?"

But Lysander continued to offer suggestions. A few of them were even helpful. By the end of the first day, Perryn was picking up the trick of using the ax's weight, instead of his own scrawny muscles, to split the wood.

As the days passed, they learned more about each other.

"You're lucky to have found a bard in Idris at all," Lysander told him. "All the smart bards have gone south, to richer kingdoms. That's what I'm doing myself, come the first cold nights."

"Running from the dragon?" Perryn swung the ax. With a sweet crack, the log split cleanly in half.

"Nice blow. Pity you don't do that more than one stroke in five. Of course I'm running from the dragon. I spent the winter in Cirin, snowed in. The dragon raided four villages in that area—pure luck it missed Cirin. When I realized that, I knew it was time for sensible men to move on. I take great pride in my good sense."

"So write a song about it," said Perryn bitterly. "How the once-great kingdom of Idris was cravenly deserted—"

"By sensible men. Why don't you come with me? You're obviously not meant to be a woodcutter, but you might find a place in one of the universities. Judging by

our conversations, you seem to be very well-read."

The ax twisted. The wood bounced.

"My father won't let me," said Perryn.

"So run away," said the bard. "That's what I always do. As soon as I'm out of here, we can—"

"When you get out of there you have to do a job for me, remember? Your oath as a bard? Write a song!"

PERRYN TRIED TO USE THE MIRROR EACH NIGHT, asking the same question. But the surface showed only his own face, except for the night when it showed Perryn's favorite riding mare, asleep in her stall. Her ears twitched and she snorted in her dreams. This might have been a reaction to his flight, but Perryn doubted it.

More days passed, and Perryn's skill grew. His arms stopped aching and got stronger. His blisters healed. He learned to work with the grain of the wood. He learned how to make the ax fall precisely where he wanted it to. He developed a rhythmic swing that ate steadily at the woodpile.

Lysander was at the window less often now. From the cell Perryn began to hear chords, fragments of melody, and an occasional, muttered curse.

Finally Perryn stood, chest heaving, before the chopping block. A small mountain of kindling rose behind him—not bad, for a scholar! Only ten logs remained. He hadn't seen Lysander since early yesterday. He hadn't heard a sound all morning.

"Lysander," he called. "Are you ready? I've done my part."

"I thought you'd never ask." The bard's mobile face popped into the window like a jumping jack. He'd charmed the guards into letting him shave regularly, though his hair was getting shaggy and his fine clothes looked bedraggled. "Mind you, the lyrics may be a little rough. I only finished them this morning."

"Let's hear it."

"And I haven't performed for some days. I may be a little rusty. Are you sure you don't want to finish up that pile while I rehearse it once or twice?"

Perryn put down the ax and folded his arms.

"All right, all right. But remember, it's rough."

The bard's face disappeared, and music took its place. The voice of the old harp was mellow and true. The swirling melody had a pronounced rhythm that was oddly familiar. Then the voice of the bard joined in and the

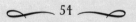

rhythm, the melody, and the words became a single entity: a song.

> *The ax is a tool*
> *For woodsmen to use*
> *Or a weapon for warriors*
> *Who'll die if they lose.*

> *Against men, against wood,*
> *When to win is the goal*
> *It's the song of the ax*
> *That's the song of your soul.*

> *The mother creates*
> *A new life with each birth.*
> *The farmer brings life*
> *From the depths of the earth.*

> *The bard strikes a string*
> *And with joy the soul fills,*
> *But the song of the ax*
> *Is a music that kills.*

The heart of the pine
Or the heart of your foe.
Both woodsman and warrior
Bring death with each blow.

Each cut jars your arm
Every stroke takes its toll,
But the song of the ax
Is the song of your soul.

The echoes sounded in Perryn's heart long after they had faded from his ears. He winced. "It's not exactly . . . heroic, is it?"

"Neither are you," said Lysander complacently.

"I suppose not." But he had his bard. That was what mattered. Perryn picked up the ax. "I'll finish here and go find the justice."

"HERE YOU ARE, LAD." THE JUSTICE'S CLERK handed him the order for Lysander's release. "All done up proper. The justice was sorry not to be here himself, but he serves all the villages in this area. When they call, he goes."

"Tell him I thank him for drawing up the order before he left," said Perryn. "And tell him . . . tell him I thank him."

"No thanks owed," said the clerk. "You worked off your friend's fine. Did a good job too. Are you quite sure you want the man? If you needed a job we could—"

"Truly? No, I'm sorry. I have to go with Lysander."

No one had ever offered him a job. It left Perryn with an astonishing sense of pride. Or not so astonishing—lowly the job might be, but he'd earned it with his own work.

"Thank you," he said. "But I can't." He left the clerk's office and was almost out of the public hall when a familiar voice from outside the door froze him in his tracks.

"I must see the justice. King's business. It's a matter of grave importance."

Cedric! Perryn backed up against a bench.

"He'll likely be in the public hall, sir," a woman replied. "And if he's not, they'll know where he is."

Perryn looked around wildly. The rows of backless benches wouldn't conceal him. The justice's big chair at the end of the room might, but it was too far away. Weapons? There was nothing but a broom leaning against the wall. He couldn't. . . .

As Cedric's tall form appeared in the doorway, Perryn

snatched up the broom, turned his back on the master of arms, and began sweeping briskly. His rough tunic was even more ragged now, after days of work and sleeping in the jail. Would Cedric be able to recognize him from behind, in strange clothing?

He listened to the footsteps as the master of arms strode down the room. They never paused.

Cedric rapped on the clerk's door and then went in.

Perryn flung down the broom and ran.

When he reached the street he spun and raced for the jail. Would Cedric reveal his business to the justice's clerk? Probably not. Cedric didn't like dealing with underlings. And even if he did, the clerk might not connect Perryn with the missing prince. But if Cedric hurried, and the clerk was alert. . . . Perryn ran faster.

"FREEDOM!" LYSANDER FLUNG HIS ARMS WIDE, gazing at the open road. "I can't wait to shake the dust of Dunstable off my feet. Why do you keep looking back? You can't be missing the place."

"They were kind to us." Perryn returned his eyes to the road ahead. "That's all."

"Speak for yourself. And that's no reason to keep spinning

around like a top. If you have another reason, don't tell me, I don't want to know. I'm enjoying myself too much. South, here I come!" He strode off so fast that Perryn had to run to catch up.

"You have a task to perform for me first, remember? That's why you're out of jail eighty-two days early."

"Very true. I am eighty-two days in your debt, and I'll pay you with pleasure. What is this task you need a true bard for?"

Perryn stopped and waited till Lysander turned to face him. "I want you to slay the dragon."

Lysander laughed.

Perryn didn't.

Lysander stopped laughing.

"Dragon's teeth! You're serious. You're crazy, but you're serious. Good-bye, Perryn. It's been nice knowing you."

"Wait!" Perryn hurried after him. "You promised to help me. You swore an oath!"

"Oaths are but words, words are but wind, and wind just blows away. An oath is made of air. The black dragon is as real as real gets. I thought you needed me to serenade your sweetheart or something!"

"Please," said Perryn urgently. "I can't make you. But

will you at least help me find a true bard who will? And a unicorn? And the Sword of Samhain?"

Lysander stopped and stared at Perryn. "I think you'd better tell me all about this. From the beginning. Take your time. Either you're crazy, or this may be the best story I'm ever going to hear."

NIGHT HAD FALLEN BY THE TIME PERRYN FINISHED. He'd decided not to tell Lysander about Cedric just yet. The dragon was enough.

"Well, I've decided," said the bard, feeding sticks into the fire he'd built in the center of their camp. "It is the best story I ever heard, and you *are* crazy!"

"But the prophecy—"

"Is probably cow flop, just like your father said. And your father is King Rovan? Of course he is. What are you then, prince muddy boots? Should I call you Your Highness?"

"Just Perryn, please." He pushed up his spectacles. He couldn't blame the bard for not believing him—Perryn couldn't imagine anyone looking less like a prince.

"On the other hand," Lysander went on, "crazy or not, I owe you something."

"So?"

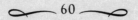

"So I'll go unicorn hunting with you. It might be interesting. And after we've failed to catch a unicorn, we'll go south and find a nice doctor to help you recover your wits."

Perryn's heart leaped. As long as Lysander agreed to help, he didn't care what the bard believed! "If we do catch a unicorn, will you go after the sword?"

"Absolutely. Why not? And once we've done that, we'll sprout our own wings and fly over the moon. But forget the dragon. By the way, how do you plan to catch this unicorn?"

"I was hoping you'd have an idea," Perryn confessed. "Aren't there songs and things about it?"

Lysander had a very unnerving smile.

"Let us proceed in our great endeavor,"
said the bard. "I know where
a unicorn might dwell."

"WHAT ELSE?" PERRYN ASKED THE GRINNING BARD.
The flickering campfire lit Lysander's face and the tips of
the branches above them.

"Pearls. Or more precisely, pearl dust. That's from *The
Ballad of the Captured Queen.* You take a whole bunch of
pearls, grind them up, and sprinkle—"

"Not that either."

"Moonstones are supposed to work. You get enough
moonstones to make a unicorn-size necklace, drop it over
their heads, and—"

"What else?"

"That one's in *The Lay of the Loving Maid.* It's a good song.
You see, this girl—"

"What else?" Perryn demanded.

"There's whitethorn seed. You dry it, grind it into powder, and blow it into the unicorn's nostrils. Of course, it doesn't say how you're supposed to get that close to the unicorn in the first place."

"You blow it into his nose? You're joking."

"It's from *The Ballad of the Revenge of the Maiden Cruelly Wronged*."

"What else?"

"I'm beginning to run out of ideas. And you rejected the best one first."

Perryn blushed. "I am not going to ask every pretty girl we meet if she's a virgin. We'd get thrown out of every town in Idris. And people would talk about it. Ced—. It isn't a good idea."

"But we could—"

"No. What else?"

"Nectar of meadow lilies?"

"Meadow lilies won't be in bloom for months. And what do you do with that? Sprinkle it on their tails?"

"Bathe their hooves with it. Then you can—"

"What else?"

"Well," said the bard. "They're supposed to like everfresh."

Perryn blinked. "Everfresh are beginning to bloom now.

They're the first flower of spring. What do you do with *them*?"

"I don't know," said the bard. "I'm out of ideas. But there are several songs that mention everfresh; unicorns lying in a field of it, or maidens picking a bunch. That kind of thing."

"Hmm. If we find a good place for a trap, maybe we could use it as bait. I suppose the songs talk about a thousand places where unicorns might be found, none of which is possible to reach?"

"They do, actually," said the bard. "With one exception. Unicorns are constantly mentioned in the forest of Wyr. There's just one problem."

"Wait. Wyr is only about a four days' walk from here. And I think the unicorn tracks I saw in that book were found in the forest of Wyr!"

"There's just one problem," the bard repeated. "Those who leave the road in the forest of Wyr never come back. It's haunted or something."

"That's ridiculous," Perryn told him.

"You're looking for a unicorn and a magic sword, and you call the curse of the forest of Wyr ridiculous? The gods may not have walked in this world for centuries, but they left a lot of magic behind, and some of it's still around.

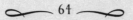

Cursed forests, as well as unicorns and swords."

"But what's the curse?"

"No one knows," the bard admitted. "It's just that no one who—"

"—leaves the road in the forest of Wyr has ever come back. So we'll set our trap near the road."

"And hope that unicorns don't avoid the only well-traveled road in the forest?"

Perryn sighed.

IN THE DAYS IT TOOK THEM TO REACH THE FOREST, Lysander proved to be a skillful traveler.

"It's illegal to trap game in the spring." Perryn eyed the rabbit sizzling on the spit hungrily.

"So arrest me, Your Highness," said the bard blandly.

Perryn shook his head. "But there's a reason for that law. Arnor, in *Bounties of Nature*, wrote that if people hunt in the spring they might catch a female, one with young to care for. If people kept doing that, soon there wouldn't be anything left to hunt."

"If people didn't trap game all year round, they'd starve," the bard argued. "With the dragon burning harvests, not to mention taking cattle and sheep, many people in Idris are going hungry. We're about out of food ourselves, in case you hadn't noticed. At the next village, I'll find a tavern to sing in."

"We'll be delayed."

"We'll be delayed worse if we start fainting from hunger. Tomorrow I'll teach you how to set a snare. No reason for me to do all the work, and the more snares you set out, the better your chances of catching something."

Perryn looked at him thoughtfully. He hoped snare setting would prove easier than chopping wood. "Game is getting scarcer, isn't it, Lysander?"

"So the old-timers tell me. Everything's scarce, in the lands where the dragon raids."

AFTER LYSANDER FELL ASLEEP THAT NIGHT, PERRYN rolled out of his blankets, pulled the mirror from his pack, and crept away from the fire's glowing embers. He'd been able to consult the mirror only a few times during their journey, since he usually fell asleep before Lysander did. Tramping the roads all day was a big change from his quiet library tower—and in some ways, dealing with Lysander was just as exhausting. He had no desire to show the skeptical bard a magic mirror that didn't work;

that would prove he was crazy.

When he got far enough away to be certain he wouldn't wake Lysander, Perryn wrapped his cloak around him to ward off the cool breeze and sat down, tilting the mirror toward the moonlight.

"Mirror of Idris, it's me, Perryn. I mean, Prince Perryndon. Show me the reaction to my flight."

He yawned, wondering why he bothered to ask that question anymore. He already knew that his father had sent Cedric to search for him. It was no wonder the mirror never troubled to answer, and he should probably quit—

Light brighter than the moon's flared from the glass, whirled and settled almost at once into a picture of his father and Cedric, seated at the big dining table—his father's alert expression made it obvious that for once the king hadn't been drinking. Judging by the sunlight pouring through the windows it was sometime in the early afternoon . . . but what day? Since his mother's death, the mirror had never moved its vision through time more than a few days, so this must have happened recently . . . or would happen soon? The mirror had been stretching its boundaries lately.

Maps and scrolls littered the table, as if his father had held a conference there. The chairs were all pushed back and hadn't yet been straightened by the servants, so his father's officers had probably just departed.

Cedric leaned forward. "There is one more matter we should consider, your Highness." His voice sounded small and distant, but the words were clear.

"Hmm?" Perryn's father scowled at the paper in his hand, some kind of list.

"It's been almost two weeks since Prince Perryndon . . . left us. Isn't it time to set a search in motion?"

Perryn frowned. People were searching for him already. Or . . . Perryn's heart sank. Had his father even been looking for him? Was Cedric searching on his own, without the king's permission? If so, it was for only one purpose. A chill ran down Perryn's spine. If Cedric was putting his energy into tracking down and assassinating the missing prince, with any luck he wouldn't have time to sabotage the kingdom's defense—but Perryn couldn't quite bring himself to be pleased about it.

"Oh, the boy. He'll come crawling back when his coin runs out."

Exasperation flashed across Cedric's face, vanishing swiftly when the king looked up at him.

"Cedric, can't we get more oats than this? We have to

keep the oxen strong, as well as the horses. The army may charge on horseback, but the oxen haul the supplies that feed the men."

"It will be attended to, Your Highness," said Cedric. "But the prince has—"

"Yes, yes, I understand," said the king. "I'm going to ask the King of Southfarthing for oats, and other supplies as well. If the Norsemen overwhelm us, Southfarthing's the next...."

The image faded, as swiftly as it had appeared.

"Thank you," said Perryn. His throat was so tight that his voice sounded hoarse. His heart felt bruised. But he wasn't going to crawl back—not ever! If his father didn't care enough to look for him, that only made it easier for him to succeed. He would return in triumph, and bring that treacherous arms master down as well!

LYSANDER SANG IN THE NEXT VILLAGE. IT MADE Perryn nervous, but it appeared that word of the prince's disappearance hadn't reached this place—and as Lysander said, they needed the money. The seven coppers he made purchased only a single bed under the attic's rafters, which Perryn shared with Lysander, and one day's food for the two of them. Perryn would rather have camped in the fields outside of town, but it began to rain soon after they reached the village, and Lysander said the damp would be bad for his voice. Since he'd earned the money, Perryn could hardly complain about how he spent it. At least, not much.

"I thought bards were richly rewarded," said Perryn as they hiked along the muddy road next morning.

"Maybe in your grandfather's time. More likely in your great-great-great-grandfather's time. Anyone who wants knowledge these days goes to a university for it, so bards aren't well paid anymore. And it's not like a university is going to travel from village to village to share its knowledge, but.... Never mind. Which king was your great-great-great-grandfather, anyway?"

"Reglin," said Perryn absently. "The fortieth warrior-king. Why be a bard then, if you don't get paid for it? For the honor?"

"I can't trip you up, can I? Come on Perryn, who are you? Really?"

"I am who I said. And you didn't answer my question. Are you a bard for the honor of it?"

Lysander snorted and picked up a stick to scrape the mud off his boots. "Bards get less honor than they do money.

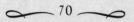

Most people think barding is just one step above begging. A short step. You go barding for the adventure," he waved his muddy stick, "to travel, to see things and meet people." He grinned suddenly. "The same reasons you go hunting for unicorns. And most of all, for the music."

"And because you promised to help me."

"Oh, that too, of course."

THE LAST VILLAGE BEFORE THE FOREST OF WYR was almost as large as a small town. Perryn collected coins in the tavern where the bard had chosen to play that night. He'd been accepted by so many people as Lysander's appren-tice that he was beginning to feel like it was true.

The tavern had been crowded when Lysander began to play, but now it was packed, and the crowd was getting rowdy. Was there any bawdy song Lysander didn't know? He'd been playing for almost three hours and hadn't repeated himself yet.

This one had a lively melody, and toes were tapping all over the room. A blacksmith, seated not far from Perryn, lurched to his feet and began to dance.

Perryn smiled. The man was drunk but no one could blame him—that lighthearted rhythm was irresistible.

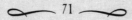

However, there really wasn't room enough for dancing, and the big smith was lurching in his direction. Lysander could collect his own coins for a while. Perryn closed their jingling purse and slipped out into the night.

The cold, fresh air felt wonderful after the tavern's stuffy heat. Perryn wandered through the inn yard and out into the street. Away from the noisy taproom the night was quiet. Everyone in the village was either at the tavern or in bed, except ... Perryn heard hoofbeats coming down the road.

He drew back toward the shadows, expecting the riders to approach the inn, but they stopped by the message board in the center of the village square. As they dismounted, Perryn saw the glitter of chain mail under their cloaks. He shrank into the bushes at the side of the road. His father's guards probably weren't the only men in Idris who wore mail, but he couldn't call any others to mind.

As Perryn watched, the two men unrolled a big sheet of paper and tacked it to the center of the board, indifferent to the other notices it covered.

They mounted their horses and rode through the village, stopping beside the inn, where a soft-voiced argument ensued. Perryn, crouched in the shadows, couldn't hear what they said. Soon they lifted their reins and rode on.

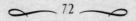

They must be camped somewhere nearby, or they'd have stopped at the tavern for the night. Perryn waited till they rounded a bend in the road, then he went quietly to the message board.

Cedric had persuaded his father to begin the hunt.

His own face stared back at him from the poster. It was a good likeness—anyone who saw it would recognize him. Ten gold pieces for information about Prince Perryndon's whereabouts, and two hundred for his safe return. His father would be furious if he had to pay out that much money. Perryn shivered. Perhaps . . . No, he wouldn't go creeping home! If he didn't prove that the prophecy was true, he'd never have any hope of earning his father's respect. *And Cedric will kill me.*

With hands that shook, Perryn reached up and pulled down the notice. He had to keep Lysander from seeing one of these. Why had he told the bard who he really was? It was too late to lie now, but as long as the bard already thought Perryn was lying he would continue with the quest. If he learned the truth. . . . Perryn crumpled the paper and went looking for the blacksmith's shop. Forge fires were kept burning all night. In a few moments the poster would be ash, and tomorrow they'd be safely into the forest of Wyr.

After that ... Perryn decided to deal with the future when it arrived.

LYSANDER MADE ENOUGH MONEY THAT NIGHT TO fill both their satchels with food. He also purchased two long coils of rope.

"If we have to leave the road for a short distance," he said, "we can tie this to a tree and be sure of getting back. Besides, it never hurts to have rope when you're hunting."

They had come south as well as east in the last few days and the weather had been warmer. Everfresh was blooming everywhere. Perryn made his cloak into a rough bag. It was full of flowers by the time they reached the outskirts of Wyr forest.

"I passed through here once." The bard peered uneasily into the green-roofed tunnel. "I didn't leave the road. No reason to. I'd forgotten how uncanny it is."

Perryn shrugged off his own uneasiness. "It's just trees. Watch for tracks like the one I drew for you. That will probably be our first sign."

He hoped he'd remembered them accurately. A good memory was one of the marks of a scholar.

Birds sang in the branches above them and small creatures

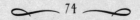

moved in the undergrowth.

"How can it be so noisy and feel so still?" Perryn murmured.

"Maybe because there's no wind." The bard didn't sound convinced.

They camped that night right in the middle of the road. Perryn made one half-hearted objection about blocking the path and then conceded. Lysander looked longingly back the way they had come.

ON THE SECOND DAY, THE ROAD CROSSED A BRIDGE over a stream and Perryn saw the first unicorn tracks. His shout of triumph echoed in the quiet wood. He leaped from the road and knelt eagerly in the soft earth beside the water. "Look, they're exactly like the picture. Exactly!"

"What makes you so sure? You said you drew it from memory." Lysander stood on the road, scowling down at him.

"It's a cloven hoof, but round instead of wedge shaped like a deer's. They're exactly like Ebron described them. What else could they be? We have to follow them!"

"Into the woods?" said the bard. "Not me, Your Highness."

"But we must! At least far enough to set a trap. You can tie your ropes to a tree and we won't leave the rope—I promise. That's what you brought them for, remember?"

"I've changed my mind."

"But it was your idea! Oh, very well, I'll go myself. Tie the ropes together. You take one end, I'll take the other, and if I get into trouble I can yank on the rope."

"If," Lysander muttered.

Perryn walked resolutely to the edge of the road, where he selected a sturdy pine and tied the end of one of the ropes to it. He tested the knot.

"Oh, all right," Lysander grumbled. "You follow the tracks and I'll follow you. I'd like to keep the road in sight if we can."

"Excellent!"

Perryn set off on the trail of the unicorn. The tracks were so clear that even an inexperienced tracker could follow them.

"I've read that unicorn magic is so strong it purifies the earth they walk on." He walked rapidly, his eyes on the ground. "These tracks look fresh. Do you think they could be? Or is some sort of—"

"I can't see the road anymore," the bard interrupted.

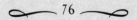

"It was there just a minute ago."

"Is your rope still tied?"

Lysander gave it a yank. "Yes." He gazed uneasily at the forest around them.

"Then stop worrying."

"Wait a moment, Perryn. I have to tie the other rope to this one."

Perryn fidgeted impatiently until the bard finished.

"The trail goes up this bank." Perryn strode on eagerly. "I wonder how much unicorns like everfresh. Watch out for a place to set a trap."

The tracks wandered up the slope, along a deer trail, and into a broad meadow with a stream running through it.

Lysander's hand closed over Perryn's collar. "Stop."

"But the trail goes—"

"We're out of rope."

"Is it still tied to the tree?"

Lysander tugged on it and nodded.

"Then just let me go into the meadow. I won't be out of sight for a moment. I'm sure these tracks are fresh."

"No." Lysander was clutching the rope so tightly his knuckles were white. "We're going back. Now."

"What is it? What's wrong?"

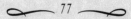

"I don't know," said the bard angrily. "If I knew I'd have told you long ago. It's like I'm hearing things I can't quite hear. I catch a glimpse of movement from the corner of my eye, but when I turn to look there's nothing there." He began to walk back, coiling the rope as fast as he could.

"I haven't seen anything."

"Except for unicorn tracks," said Lysander. "You wouldn't have seen a dragon unless you tripped over it. Are you coming or not?"

Perryn looked at the tracks leading into the meadow. Now that he noticed it, even the sunlit field felt haunted. He turned and followed the bard.

None of the trees looked familiar. If it hadn't been for the rope and the tracks, Perryn would have sworn they were going the wrong way. He listened for the sound of the stream but he didn't hear it.

Lysander came to a stop. His sweaty face was pale, his expression grim.

"What is it?" Perryn looked past him, and at last he saw a tree he recognized—a sturdy pine. Lysander's rope was tied to it. The road was nowhere in sight.

"Courage," said Prince Perryndon.
"We may have missed the road, but we are not lost.
The prophecy guides us."

6

"IT'S ENTIRELY MY OWN FAULT," SAID LYSANDER. "I knew you were crazy. Why did I follow you? Why? Why me? No, it's *your* fault."

"Me? You're the bard. You're the one who's supposed to know about this forest. And tying the rope to the tree was your idea!"

"How was I to know that the trees moved?"

Exhausted tears burned in Perryn's eyes and he pulled off his spectacles to rub them. At least it was too dark for the bard to see him. "I still don't believe it," he muttered.

"Either the trees moved or the road did. And the unicorn tracks, too. Can any of your books explain that?"

"Maybe somewhere," said Perryn, trying to control

the quiver in his voice. "But if there's a book that does, I haven't read it."

They had followed the tracks backward until they ran into a grove of trees so dense they couldn't get through. When they circled around it, they found no trace of unicorn tracks on the other side.

With no other course available to them, they followed the tracks back to the meadow with the stream. The sun was low when they reached it, clearly indicating which direction was west. They had entered the forest on the west side and moved east, so they decided to walk toward the sunset. They walked in a straight line for more than three hours.

Perryn noticed unicorn tracks again and again. In spite of himself he began to follow them with his eyes, though his feet still followed the bard, until Lysander stepped out of the forest into a wide meadow with a stream running through it—a meadow they'd already seen twice. It felt strange, to hate the sight of such a beautiful place.

"There are worse things than tears," said Lysander gently. "I have a cousin who used to cry, and he outgrew it."

"When he was fourteen?" demanded Perryn. "I hate myself when I cry. But I can't seem to help it." He turned away.

"I have an idea," said Lysander. "Suppose we follow the

stream. It will flow into something else eventually, maybe even the stream that crosses the road. We'll have water, and if we're lucky with snares, or perhaps catch a fish or two, we'll have food for about four days. We'd make it. All we have to do is follow the stream."

"Unless it flows into a lake with no outlet. Or in a circle."

Lysander opened his mouth to say that a stream couldn't flow in a circle, then shut it.

"But I'll bet," Perryn continued, "that if the stream flows out of the forest, the trees won't let us follow it."

"If you have a better idea, then by all means share it."

"I think I do," said Perryn hesitantly. "The unicorn tracks don't seem to be moving. I think that's why the trees planted themselves so thickly in that one grove, because they had to cover them up."

"So?"

"There are unicorn tracks all over this wood. And they're creatures of magic, so they might be able to defeat the magic of the forest."

"Dragon's teeth!" the bard exclaimed. "You still want to hunt unicorns? We only have enough food for a few days!"

"Others have been lost in this forest," Perryn pointed out.

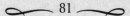

"Some of them must have followed the stream. Has anyone ever escaped?"

Lysander began to reply, but evidently no one had, because he stopped.

"All I'm saying is that we ought to try something different," Perryn continued. "Something that hasn't failed already."

"Catching a unicorn to lead you out would certainly be different." The bard thought it over. Perryn waited.

"Very well," said Lysander finally. "We'll spend two days trying to catch a unicorn. But if we haven't succeeded by then, we try the stream while we still have some food. We need to spend the rest of the night here, though. I'm so tired I'm reeling. Agreed?"

"Agreed." Perryn nodded happily. "I have an idea for a trap already."

"Good." Lysander yawned. "Because if we should catch a unicorn, and it won't lead us out, something that large could extend our food supply for a long time."

Perryn's outraged yelp was answered by a snore.

LATER THAT NIGHT, PERRYN CREPT AWAY FROM THE sleeping bard. Catching a unicorn might work, but perhaps there was a simpler way. It wouldn't hurt to try.

"Mirror of Idris, I am Perryndon, Prince of Idris. Show me the way out of this wood."

Perryn held his breath—surely this was something he needed to know!

The mirror flickered. Then, as if Perryn's hope had willed it into being, an image emerged.

He was looking down from the battlements of Idris Castle, and the army was marching out below him. They were leaving to fight the Norse!

As if following Perryn's desire, the mirror focused on the man who rode at the head of the column, and Perryn's heart swelled with pride.

Grave and commanding, the king was talking to a man who rode beside him, nodding respectfully. King Rovan's armor was better made than that of the men who followed him, but no gold adorned it, and it showed the scars of mending. The king might drink too deeply, but he served his kingdom well, standing against the Norsemen summer after summer, defending us all.

No wonder he was so disappointed in his scholarly son. He deserved—

"The king should be allowed to concentrate on important matters." Cedric's voice rose softly from the mirror as the image spun and shifted to the master of arms, who stood on the battlements watching the king ride off to war. The head of the palace guard stood beside him. "If you should get word of the prince, come to me before you send any messengers to His Highness. He shouldn't be distracted from the campaign. Do you understand?"

"Yes, sir," said the guard.

The vision faded, leaving Perryn chilled with fear—but exasperated as well. How many times had he asked to see his father only to be shown nothing, or something completely irrelevant, and now. . . . Though he had to admit, Cedric's order was something he *needed* to know. He couldn't approach any of his father's guard. No matter what he told them, they'd turn him over to the master of arms.

However, not even Cedric could find him here. Perryn was perfectly safe . . . except from wandering in circles until he starved to death. He rose wearily to his feet and went back to Lysander. Tomorrow they'd start hunting for a unicorn.

IN THE MORNING, PERRYN FOUND THE TRACKS easily.

"You see? Dozens of tracks. Unicorns must use this path all the time."

"Hmm," said the bard. "The trees don't seem to be changing anymore. You don't suppose..."

"No," said Perryn. "I think they'd start to move as soon as we tried to get out."

"You mean they know our intentions? But that's insa— What a horrible thought."

"Come on," said Perryn. "Let's see if we can find a place for a trap."

IT WAS SIMPLE—TWO LARGE SNARE LOOPS, attached to springy young trees that had been bent almost to the ground. The loops were held slack with a single stake, pounded into the soft soil just deeply enough to hold the trees down.

"We cover the loops with dead leaves," Perryn explained. "And hide in the bushes till the unicorn steps into the loops. Then we pull the stakes, the trees spring up, the loops go tight..."

"I understand. I taught you how to set a snare, remember? What makes you think a unicorn will step into the loops?"

"For one thing they're set right across the trail. For another..."

Perryn went over to the snare and opened his cloak, dumping a pile of everfresh to the ground. The blossoms were slightly crushed, but their sweet scent filled the air.

"If you say so," said the bard sourly.

"Come on," said Perryn. "Let's hide. One of them could come along at any moment."

IT WAS THE MOST BORING DAY OF PERRYN'S LIFE. He couldn't see Lysander, much less speak with him. His bruises and scrapes ached. Insect bites itched.

As the sun crawled across the sky he had time to imagine everything that could possibly go wrong, and some things that couldn't. It helped him stay awake. He hoped Lysander was awake, but he wouldn't have bet a cracked copper on it—much less his life.

The first stars of evening were blooming in the sky when the unicorn appeared; Perryn's breath caught at its beauty. It was the size of a small pony, and its white coat glowed in the gathering dusk as if it were made of moonlight. Its hooves gleamed. It hesitated a moment, nostrils widening as it sniffed the air. Then it moved gracefully toward the trap.

Perryn's heart thudded in his throat and his palms were damp. A few paces from the trap the unicorn hesitated again. Then it reached down daintily, hooked the snare loops with the tip of its horn, and tossed them aside. It stepped into the everfresh and bent its head, inhaling deeply.

Perryn leaped to his feet with a shout, tripped over the stake, and fell flat. Branches thrashed and the rope hissed above his head as the tree sprang upright. He heard the bard crashing through the bushes across from him as he scrambled toward the trap.

The unicorn waited till Lysander had almost reached it, then it cleared the everfresh with a single, agile bound and sprang down the path.

A laugh like silver chimes rang, not in Perryn's ears, but in his mind. He shook his head and ran down the trail after Lysander and the unicorn.

It led them on a chase. Over rocks, through streams, and in and out of thorny bushes. It vaulted over mud puddles Perryn and the bard had to wade through. Perryn was about to give up when the unicorn came to a skidding stop. Before it lay a patch of bog, too wide to cross with a single leap.

With a cry of triumph Lysander surged forward.

The unicorn glared at the bog, then gathered its muscles and leaped, just as Lysander jumped for it. It lit on a small hummock and teetered precariously.

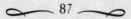

Lysander fell into the bog, launching a sheet of liquid mud in all directions. The high-pitched shriek in Perryn's mind made his head ache. With a final, nimble leap the unicorn fled, its spotless white hide shining in the dark.

Perryn pulled the bard out of the mud and waited until the stream of curses ran out. "At least we learned something," he remarked. "Alirian the teacher wrote that no experiment is a failure if you learn from it."

"What have we learned? That unicorns are both faster and smarter than we are?"

"It hates mud," said Perryn. "Look at us. It didn't have a spot on it. It almost let you catch it rather than risk falling into that muck."

"I'm not thrilled about it myself." The bard wiped his muddy hands on his muddy tunic and grimaced. "And what was that . . . it wasn't a sound, exactly."

"I think it must have been a mind-voice," Perryn said. "I've read that many magical creatures possess them, and even the mir—even some man-made artifacts were given voices by their creators, so they could communicate with others. But I'd never heard one before."

In fact, he'd never dreamed he might hear one, and the thrill of it pulsed in his heart. He'd read that powerful magic was always self-aware and usually possessed some means to give that awareness voice. And magic was what he needed to defeat the dragon!

"Come on," said Perryn. "I have another plan."

THE UNICORN WAS MORE CAUTIOUS THE NEXT night, pausing frequently to smell the breeze and peer about. Perryn had taken care to be downwind of the starting point of his trap. The swamp mud reeked.

The unicorn came slowly down the path and passed his hiding place. Perryn waited till it had almost reached the sharp bend before he leaped out.

"Got you!" he shouted. He ran toward it, swinging a mud-drenched strip of what remained of his cloak. With a mind-splitting shriek the unicorn darted down the trail—just as Perryn had hoped it would! The next shriek, as the unicorn almost collided with the mud-soaked rags he had hung across the path, was even shriller. Perryn was almost on it now. Mud-soaked rags ahead, mud-covered grass and roots draping the bushes to the left, and the mud-drenched boy behind. The unicorn bolted right.

It had taken most of the day to find a place to set this trap, but now the unicorn was racing down a closed chute, the

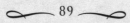

89

long, wide bog on its left and a wall of muddy bushes on its right. They had sacrificed Perryn's cloak, all of Lysander's spare clothes, and one of the ropes to make a solid fence. Unless the unicorn was prepared to get dirty, there was only one direction it could go.

And it was going that way with amazing speed. Perryn was barely able to stay close enough to see the culmination of his plan.

The bog curved. Now the unicorn saw the bog to the right and ahead of it, mud-wrapped bushes to the left, and the muddy boy behind. One of the bushes was lower than the others. With a mighty leap, the unicorn left the ground. It cleared the low bush with inches to spare and lit right in the center of the snare loop. Branches thrashed as the rope whipped around the unicorn's neck.

Lysander grabbed the other end of the rope, keeping it taut so the unicorn couldn't slip out of it. "Got you, you slippery moon beam."

Perryn squirmed through the brush.

The unicorn's sides heaved. Its eyes rolled up and it slid limply to the ground.

"Of course I will aid so noble a cause,"
said the unicorn.

7

"NOW WHAT?" PERRYN GAZED AT THE UNCONSCIOUS unicorn—he had no idea what to do.

"Hobbles," said the bard, snatching up the remainder of their first rope. "As fast as we can make them." He had barely bound the creature's back feet when it began to stir.

"Ooh, what a horrible dream." The voice chimed in Perryn's mind. "I dreamed—*Eek!*"

Perryn winced, clapping his hands to his temples. "Please, don't do that." Nothing he'd ever read had mentioned how *loud* a mind-voice could be.

"Stay away from me you . . . monsters!"

"Don't be afraid," said Perryn. "We need your help. We won't do anything to you—"

"Provided you do as we ask," Lysander said firmly.

The unicorn struggled to her feet and turned her head, examining her pristine hide. There wasn't a speck of dirt on her. She took a couple of halting steps in the hobbles, and sighed.

"I suppose I must help you, if I wish to be free. What is it you want?"

"A guide," said the bard. "Can you lead us out of the forest?"

"As a bard, sir, you should know that. I am a creature of magic, so the curse of the wood doesn't affect me."

"How did you know I was a bard?" asked Lysander suspiciously.

"By the harp you're carrying. Just as I know by his gentle manner that this . . ." She grimaced. "This filthy person is noble born. How should I address you, noble sir? I would hate to do so improperly."

"Call me Perryn. My friend's name is Lysander. And you are?"

"My name is Prism," the unicorn's voice chimed in his head. "And I will gladly lead you from the forest if you'll free my feet. Not you, Perryn," she added quickly. "Lysander, if you please. He's cleaner."

"How do we know you won't run off?" Lysander demanded.

"Sir! I have given you my word. The unicorn's creed demands that once you have given your word it cannot be broken. I may be less than a hundred years old, but I am a unicorn, pure of thought, word, and deed. I would never do such a thing."

Lysander snorted. "You can walk to the edge of the forest in hobbles. And if you try to run off we'll grind up your horn and sell it for love potions."

"Ooh!" Prism's eyes rolled up.

"No, we won't," said Perryn. "Don't faint! We won't let any harm come to you."

Prism's eyes returned to normal. She swayed unsteadily for a moment, then recovered.

"You swear you won't harm me?"

"You have my oath. I may not be as clean as you'd like, but I keep my promises," Perryn answered.

"Very well, noble sir. Free me and I will lead you out."

"Ah . . . there's one more thing," said Perryn. "I'm on sort of a quest. Fulfilling a prophecy. And it calls for a unicorn."

"Prophecies often mention unicorns," Prism boasted. "We have a proud history of assisting in quests, because of our healing powers and our courage. The great ones, in the age of heroes, often sought out a unicorn to be their steed when they … you don't want me to do anything *dangerous*, do you?"

"No," said Perryn quickly. "Just heal us if we fall ill."

"Oh, I can do that," said Prism. "Unicorns can cure the dragon's wrath, the fever that comes when a dragon's blood mingles with the blood of a man, and lesser illnesses are even easier to deal with. I can't do anything about wounds, mind you, because they're an injury instead of a corruption of the body. But if you happen to fall ill while on your quest, I will certainly heal you. You have my word."

"Very well. Let her go, Lysander."

"But what if—"

"Do it."

"Humph," said Prism as Lysander bent to the hobbles. "You obviously know nothing about unicorns. Some bard you are."

LYSANDER MUTTERED DARKLY WHEN PRISM LED them north.

"It's the quickest way out of the forest," she told him. "That's what you said you wanted."

And sure enough, by the end of the day the trees began to thin and the eerie feeling lessened.

94

"The magic is weaker here," Prism told them. "The trees can only move slowly. In fact, this would be a good place to stop for the night. We'll probably be surrounded when we wake up but I can lead you out easily, and that way we can pass by the black bog in the daylight."

"The black bog?" Lysander's voice scaled up. "You led us to the death-sleep marsh?"

"Near to it," said Prism apologetically. "But, we'll go around, I assure you. It's very dirty." She shivered.

"In *Polidanus on Potions* I read that the black bog never does anything except make people sleep," said Perryn. "Didn't people use the water for sleeping potions?"

"They did," Lysander admitted. "But the water also makes you sleep if it touches your skin. Too many people came for a sleeping potion, got their feet wet, and fell in and drowned. Sometimes in just a few inches of water, because no one dared to pull them ashore lest they be splashed. That's how it got its reputation. And why no one in their right mind goes there now." He glared at Prism.

"Don't be so timid," said the unicorn. "If it weren't muddy, I could purify the water for hundreds of yards. Maybe even the entire swamp. But since you're afraid, I'll take you around it."

"But we could still get some of the water," said Perryn. "Couldn't we?"

"Trouble sleeping?" the bard asked ironically. "Death will cure insomnia, that's for sure. Are you out of your mind?"

"Who knows what we'll face when we go looking for the Sword of Samhain? A sleeping potion might be useful."

"Why are you two looking for the Sword of Samhain?" Prism asked curiously.

"Dragon's teeth! You're not going on with this prophecy foolishness, are you? We almost got killed in that forest!" Lysander said.

"But we didn't," said Perryn. "And we found a unicorn. The prophecy is coming true, Lysander! Can't you see it? With Prism to purify the marsh water, what risk is there?"

"You want me to go into the black bog? All that mud? Never!" Prism sprang to her feet.

The bard tackled her as she leaped for the forest.

"BUT YOU DON'T UNDERSTAND!" PRISM WAILED. Her hooves skidded in the soft earth as Perryn and Lysander dragged her onward. "It isn't just the mud. I'll be darkened. I'll start to vanish!"

Her shoulder slammed into Perryn and he slipped on the spongy ground and almost fell. Only his grasp on the unicorn's neck saved him.

Prism had fainted when Lysander caught her. Perryn and the bard had carried the unconscious unicorn to the very edge of the marsh before she came to. She was curiously light for a creature her size, but her struggles were mighty.

"You'd get less dirty if you stopped fighting, you stupid jackass," the bard complained, pushing her from behind.

"We're not asking you to do anything except save us if we fall in," Perryn argued, pulling on her mane. "You promised us—"

"I agreed to heal you," Prism panted. "No one said anything about saving." She bucked. The bard tottered and yelped again.

"But you're in no danger," Perryn protested. "You can purify the water—it can't hurt you."

"That's what you think!"

Prism's head went down and her back legs lashed out. The bard yelped. There was an enormous splash, then silence.

Perryn pushed past the unicorn to where the bard had

stood. The shallow pool, mere inches deep, had been concealed by the reeds. The bard lay in it, unmoving . . . face down.

"Lysander!" Perryn started forward.

"Don't!" A spiraled horn barred his path, like a guardsman's lance. "He's soaked. You'd only fall asleep yourself."

"But he'll drown! Maybe I can pull him out with a stick." Perryn glanced around frantically, but he saw nothing large enough to serve the purpose.

Prism shivered delicately and stepped into the water. The ripples that spread from her dainty hooves caught the moonlight like mirrors.

She bent her neck and dipped her horn into the pool, thrusting it beneath the bard's unconscious body. With a graceful heave she lifted her head. The bard slid down her neck and back into the water.

Perryn reached for him.

"No." Prism lowered her head again. This time the bard's limp body fell over her withers. Prism waited until his weight settled, then walked carefully out of the swamp. A quick shake slid Lysander off her back. She reached down and touched his throat with the tip of her horn. The bard's lungs heaved, and he choked and began to cough.

 98

"You can touch him now." Prism moved a few paces away, her head bowed.

Lysander's coughs were interspersed with curses. He seemed to be recovering, so Perryn followed the unicorn.

"What is it, Prism? What's wrong?"

"Where is it?" asked the unicorn.

"Where's what?"

"The dark spot."

"But you hardly got dirty at all." Perryn brushed a few flecks of mud from her coat. One spot refused to yield and Perryn looked closer. A gray dapple the size of a thumbprint marked her right wither, and it wasn't dirt.

"That wasn't there before, was it?"

"No," said Prism. "I had managed to avoid situations that ... that demanded action on my part." She turned her head to study the dapple sadly.

"I don't understand," said Perryn.

"I suppose not. Have you ever wondered why unicorns are so seldom seen? You saw the tracks of dozens of unicorns in the forest, but you saw only me."

"I thought ... I guess I never thought about it."

"The reason you didn't see the others is because the older unicorns are grayed. Spotted like this all over. The more spots, the less white, the harder they are for humans to see. Some very old unicorns are nearly black." Prism shuddered. "Even other unicorns can barely see them. When a unicorn becomes wholly black, it's gone forever."

Gone. Did she mean death, or something else? No wonder she didn't like getting dirty! None of the books he'd read had ever mentioned any of this. Perryn groped for the right words.

"If it's just, well, part of getting older..."

"It isn't," said Prism. "You get dark spots only when you do good deeds. That's how unicorn magic works. When you purify something you draw the evil and corruption into yourself, and because impurity cannot live in a unicorn, it vanishes. But it leaves a spot like that." She looked at the dapple and winced.

"Then I'd think you'd be proud of it."

"Of course, the darker the unicorn, the more it's respected." Prism eyed the dapple more tolerantly. "It is the honorable destiny of unicorns to darken. In fact, some have accused me of shirking my duty. Maybe they won't be so condescending now." Then she shuddered again. "But to vanish? To get darker and darker until you're obliterated?"

"Then why did you promise to heal us?" Lysander joined

them, still dripping and blinking sleepily.

Prism hung her head. "You both looked so healthy. I thought you might get hurt on your quest, but I didn't think you were likely to fall ill or get poisoned. The truth is, I didn't think I'd have to do anything."

"Will you still come with us?" Perryn asked.

"Certainly." Prism looked shocked. "I gave my word. Besides, you have a prophecy. It doesn't say anything about the unicorn getting hurt, does it?"

"No," said Perryn. "It doesn't say whether anyone gets hurt. Only that we'll succeed."

"You promised I wouldn't have to do anything danger-ous." Prism sounded calmer now. "And you're unlikely to get sick again. By the way, what does the prophecy say we're going to do?"

Perryn hesitated, but there was no use putting it off. "We're going to slay the dragon."

Prism fainted.

"The sword was placed in the tomb of my ancestor,"
said Prince Perryndon. "It is part of my history,
my heritage. I know where it lies."

8

WITH THE AID OF A LONG BRANCH, PERRYN FINALLY
succeeded in filling a flask with water from the black bog.

"I still can't think why you want the stuff," said Lysander.
They were waiting for the outside of the flask to dry so
Perryn could handle it. "Not to mention the fact that now
you have nothing in which to carry your drinking water."

"I've been thinking about it," said Perryn. "The stream
that fills this marsh comes out of the forest. I'll bet the sleepi-
ness in this water should be part of the trees, but the magic
of the forest drains it out of them and into the water. That's
why the trees are so lively and the water makes you sleep."

"You may be right," said the bard. "So what?"

"Well, Malthin the sorcerer wrote that the only way to
fight a magical creature is with magic. That's why I started

doing research, to find some kind of magic that might work against the dragon—but there wasn't much. So it seems to me that if I find something magical, I ought to use it. Or try to, anyway."

"But if dragons could be defeated with magic, then wouldn't the Norse just defeat them, instead of... appeasing them, the way they do?" Lysander asked.

"I've thought about that, too," said Perryn. "We know that the Norse claim to have more control over magic than we do, but if that's true why don't they use it against our army? So I think the rumor that they're controlling the dragon must be exaggerated."

"I don't know," said Lysander. "And since I never intend to get within five miles of any Norsemen, I don't much care. Just remember, if we come to the dragon part, I'm leaving."

"I think it makes a great deal of sense," said Prism. "You say the next thing we need is the Sword of Samhain? Where do we go for that?"

"It's in the tomb of Albion, the twenty-seventh warrior-king," said Perryn, gingerly capping his flask. "Lysander will know where that is."

"I will?" said Lysander.

"You mean you don't? I thought all the songs about the

warrior-kings' deaths talked about their burials!"

"Certainly. They tell about the speeches people made, and who was there, and even what they wore and ate, but for some reason they never give you explicit directions to the barrow. Haven't you ever heard of grave robbers, Your Highness?"

"None of my books said anything about grave robbers," Perryn protested. He was beginning to wonder if the information in his library tower was as complete as he had once believed.

"That settles that," said the bard. "We can't find the barrow, we can't find the sword, we can't fulfill the prophecy. Let's go south."

"No," said Perryn.

"Do you know where the barrow is?"

"No, but I think I can find out. Let's camp here tonight."

PRISM SLEPT MORE LIGHTLY THAN LYSANDER, BUT finally Perryn was able to take the mirror aside and rest its cool weight on his lap.

"Mirror of Idris," he whispered, "will you show me the location of King Albion's tomb?"

A familiar image flashed to the surface—a road, with

another, smaller track branching off into the low, scrub-covered hills. It was day in the image this time, but it was the same fork in the road Perryn had seen before. And it was still empty.

Perryn frowned. How could this be important? It certainly wasn't the location of King Albion's tomb, for none of the kings was buried near any roads. After Lysander talked about tomb robbers, Perryn had realized *why* all the barrows were located in isolated hills and valleys.

"Thank you," he told the mirror politely. The image of the empty road lingered for a moment before it faded. But the mirror's failure left only one other option—his library.

On one hand, at least Perryn's father wouldn't be there. On the other hand, Cedric and the guards would. But if neither the mirror nor Lysander could help him, Perryn had no choice. He had to go home.

"YOU'RE GOING TO BREAK INTO IDRIS CASTLE? This is carrying your fantasy of being a prince too far. They'll hang us by the thumbs when we get caught!" said Lysander.

"No, they won't." Perryn pushed a low branch out of the way. The shortcut through the woods to the castle was

somewhat overgrown. "I'll tell them you were protecting me and that you tricked me into coming back. My father will probably reward you."

"How much? Oh, all right. I suppose I might convince them that I believed your story about being Prince Perryndon, though that's pretty thin—but what would they do to you?"

"Nothing," said Perryn. "Oh, I suppose the guards would lock me in my room till my father gets back. But if I'm imprisoned, that will mean the end of the prophecy!" And possibly his death, if Cedric could contrive his "accident" before the king returned. The one good thing about this was that Idris Castle was the last place Cedric would expect to find him.

Perryn had asked the mirror for the location of King Albion's tomb several times on the four days' journey back to the castle but it had shown him nothing, except once, when he'd seen an old man on a stream bank fishing for trout. He shouldn't ask too much of the mirror, he reminded himself. They had to do this. Though if Cedric caught him . . .

"I'd say good riddance to the prophecy," said Lysander. "Except that it would also be the end of us."

"Be quiet," said Perryn. "We're almost out of the trees. The guards might hear us."

"And they might shoot before they discover who you are," said Prism uneasily. "I'm not sure this is such a good idea."

The bard came to a stop, looking over the cleared space that surrounded the castle. "I never noticed how formidable it is. Prissy-prim is right. We'll all get shot crossing the cleared ground."

"No, we won't," said Perryn confidently. "I crossed it when I ran away with no trouble and the moon was brighter then. Besides, I thought you liked adventure."

"Adventure is one thing, suicide is another." Lysander insisted. "You didn't have a snow-white unicorn with you before. The guards would have to be stone blind not to see her. Unicorn soup was a delicacy in the elder days, wasn't it?"

"No," said Perryn. "Stop doing that. Prism, take deep breaths and try to calm down. You have to learn not to faint, before we go against the drag—. Take a deep breath, and hold your head down! There, that's better."

He had wondered what they would do with Prism, traveling on the road, but the unicorn displayed an amazing ability to hide herself whenever they heard someone approaching. Crossing an open meadow on a clear night, that wouldn't be an option.

"Much use she'll be," said the bard. "If we're really going to do this, we'd better leave her here."

"You're right," said Perryn. "She does show up in the dark, and we don't have any garments left that are big enough to cover her. Though we could rub her with dirt. I think you'd better stay here, Prism."

"Gladly," said the unicorn. "How long shall I wait? I mean, not to be indelicate, but suppose you don't come back?"

"Wait till morning," said Perryn. "We should be back long before then. Lysander, get ready to run when that guard walks away. Keep low and stay in the bushes.

"Yes, Your Highness," said the bard sardonically. "What were you really when you worked here? A stable boy? Kitchen—"

"Now!" Perryn darted off, Lysander scrambling at his heels.

It took longer without the wind-blown clouds that had aided Perryn's escape, but they reached the base of the wall without being seen. The guards in the parapet above them would have to lean far over the edge to see them now.

"I have to talk to my father about this," Perryn murmured. "We keep such a careful watch for the dragon that anyone could get into this place from the ground."

"We're not in yet," the bard whispered back. "How do you propose to get through the wall? Scuttle through the cracks like rats?"

"Exactly." Perryn moved down the wall. He might have missed the low grating, if his feet hadn't sunk into the mud.

"It's here." He knelt and quietly began pulling up clumps of grass. "It's a sewer, a small stream that runs right under the castle. The grating is almost rusted away. Father keeps talking about replacing it, but he never does. That's what made me think of it."

"The *old* sewer, I hope? It hasn't been used in years?"

"Sorry," said Perryn. "But this is the side that flows into the castle so it shouldn't be too bad." The bars of the grating hardly made a sound as they broke under his hands.

"You didn't come out this way," the bard observed softly.

Perryn shook his head. He took off his spectacles and tucked them into his belt pouch.

"Then why aren't we going in the same way you came out, Your Highness?"

"Because they pulled up the blankets. Follow me."

Perryn lowered himself into the mud and wiggled through the opening.

The sewer culvert seemed very long. At times the mud was so deep that Perryn had to turn his head sideways against the ceiling to keep his mouth above the water. Finally his searching fingers touched dry stone, with open space beyond, and he pulled himself out onto the cold floor.

There was no light at all. Perryn took out his spectacles, rinsed them in the stream, and put them on, but he still couldn't see anything except darkness. He heard splashing as the bard struggled free of the culvert, and groped for his hands to help him out.

"It's a good thing we didn't try to bring Prism with us," said Perryn. His mud-soaked clothes clung to his body.

"Where are we?" the bard demanded. "I can't see a thing. How are we going to get out of here?"

"Find a wall and follow it," Perryn told him. "This corridor goes straight to the wine cellar stairs. But don't go through any doors. This is the old dungeon and there are oubliettes in some of the cells. Most of the trapdoors are pretty rotten too."

"What a nasty thought." The bard groped for a wall.

"No one's been dropped into them for, oh, centuries now,"

said Perryn. "And even in the old days, Idris' kings were more inclined to chop peoples' heads off than to starve them to death."

"How do you know all this?" Lysander asked. "Were you a clerk here?"

Perryn sighed. "It's the easiest way into the castle."

"Then why did Your Highness have to climb down blankets?"

"Personal reasons. Are you afraid of rats?"

"Not particularly."

"Good, because I am. You go first."

There *were* rats. Perryn could hear them, scuttling away from the noise of their footsteps. Claws scratched on the stone flags and small bodies rustled in the dark. Sweat broke out on his muddy face. There must be hundreds of them! He ran into the bard's back.

"What are you doing? We have to keep moving! They'll come if we're quiet." Perryn stamped his feet furiously.

"Don't make such a fuss," said the bard. "It's only a few rats. I've run into the stairs but I can't find a railing."

"There probably isn't one; this is the oldest part of the castle. Get going!"

The bard hesitated a long moment before starting up the

dark stairs. The rats seemed to grow fewer as they climbed, but Perryn was shaking when they reached the top.

"No more steps," said Lysander.

"Th-this is the wine cellar." Perryn's teeth were chattering. "Keep following the wall."

"You really are afraid of rats, aren't you?" A hollow thud echoed softly. "Ah." The bard sounded pleased. "Wine barrel. You were right. I've been here before." He moved faster, thumping the barrels as he went.

"I know; I heard about it. Were you really down here stealing the wine?"

"Just a few bottles," said Lysander. "The steward here is a most miserly man. I mean, even if the king wasn't in residence to hear me play, this is the palace! And I should have been paid accordingly."

"But why wine? I don't think I've ever seen you drink more than a mug of beer—and not often even that." Accustomed to the amount his father drank, the bard's abstinence seemed almost unnatural to Perryn.

"Drinking's bad for the voice," said Lysander. "But low pay is bad for the whole bard! Bad for all bards, everywhere, if you let them get away with it. I regard it as my duty to my craft brothers to—hold up."

Perryn bumped into his back. "What is it?"

"I've found the door." A soft rattle sounded. "But it's locked. It wasn't locked the last time."

"Someone must have decided to take a few precautions against wandering bards," said Perryn. "What are we going to do? If we wait for someone to open the door in the morning, Prism will be gone."

"Don't worry."

Perryn heard the bard fumbling in the darkness, then a scraping sound. "What are you doing?"

"Nothing much. But since stewards take precautions against crafty bards, a bard must take steps to thwart miserly stewards. There!"

A sharp click sounded and the door swung open. The dim light of the kitchen fires seemed bright as it washed into the black cellar. The bard slipped a small, gleaming tool into his belt.

"Lock pick?"

Lysander grinned. "Just a precaution. After you, Prince Perryndon."

The scullery boy sleeping in the kitchen didn't stir as they tiptoed past. Perryn peered into the great hall. It was empty of guards since the king was gone. Would his father be proud if he could see Perryn now?

No, not proud. Furious. But fulfilling the prophecy matters more than what Father thinks of me.

The thought startled Perryn so much that he stopped in his tracks, and Lysander ran into him and whispered a curse. He moved forward once more, but the sudden revelation lingered. Fulfilling the prophecy *did* matter more. Perryn had always known that—but it hadn't been true in his heart, until now.

Was it coming back to his home that had made the difference? Something else? Whatever it was, Perryn didn't have time to think about it now. He crept on down the corridor until he reached the stairs to the library tower and peeked cautiously around the corner. Then he gestured for Lysander to follow him and hurried upward.

"Dragon's teeth," the bard breathed, staring into one of the cluttered, paper-strewn rooms. "You'll never find anything in this mess. It would take years."

"It did," Perryn told him. "I'm going to organize it someday. But I remember almost exactly where the book with the location of the king's tomb is. Here, in this room. And I think there's a map in here that shows the road to the dragon's valley as well."

Lysander followed him in. "Don't you need light?"

"We don't dare light a candle," said Perryn, scanning the shelves of books and scrolls. "I'm the only one who ever comes here, so anyone who sees it would be bound to investigate. There's enough moonlight to read by, if I can . . . ah, this is it."

He carried the heavy book over to the window, perched it on the sill, and began flipping pages. "Twenty-third king, laws made . . . Twenty-fourth king . . . Twenty-sixth king, coronation . . . Here it is! Twenty-seventh king, buried." He read rapidly. "Lysander, this is wonderful! The tomb of the twenty-seventh king is in the foothills, in the same direction as the dragon's lair! We'll hardly have to go out of our way at all."

He turned to the bard.

Lysander stared at him, an odd expression on his face. "You really are Prince Perryndon, aren't you? You really are!"

Then they sought the Sword of Samhain.
The noblest weapon in the history
of Idris.

9

"I CAN'T BELIEVE YOU'RE REALLY PRINCE PERRYNDON!" the bard exclaimed, for perhaps the dozenth time.

He had said it when they slipped into Perryn's room to get some warm winter clothing and another water flask. He had said it as they crawled out through the narrow sewer, rejoined Prism, and hiked several exhausting miles past the borders of the castle lands. And now, as they sat around the fire and dried their wet, muddy clothes, he was still saying it.

"I knew it at once," Prism told the bard. "Anyone with such a gentle manner, who showed such courtesy—and under some very adverse circumstances, I might add—"

"I know, I know," the bard grumbled. "Noble born and all that. But I still can't believe—"

"Let's talk about what we're going to do next," said

Perryn hastily. "If we're going to rob a tomb we'll need picks and shovels and things, won't we?"

"Why didn't you get them at the castle?" asked Prism. "You brought lots of other things." She gazed disdainfully at the damp, woolen clothes that festooned the bushes.

"Too big," Perryn told her. "Getting the clothes, the book, and the map out was hard enough, but we had to have them." He wrapped his arms around himself, but the chill he felt had little to do with the cold night air. Seeing the heavy bolt Cedric had fastened on the door of his room had shaken him.

"What book?"

Perryn fished the slim volume out of its canvas wrapping. "*Medicinal Uses of the Waters of the Black Bog.* I thought I remembered seeing it."

"That's the first time I've heard you talk about a book without mentioning the author," said Lysander.

"It's anonymous."

"How very reassuring."

"Don't worry, lots of the old books are anonymous. It talks about dosage, but not for anything as big as a dragon. Maybe I can boil it down, to concentrate it. And I was right when I said that black-bog water never killed anyone."

"No wonder it's anonymous—he's wrong. The black bog has killed dozens of people."

"Only when they fell in and drowned. This tells about a little girl who accidentally drank too much of it and slept for five weeks. They poked a hollow reed down her throat to feed her so she wouldn't starve, and when she woke up she was fine."

"But why did you bring the map and the laundry?" Prism asked.

"We'll need winter clothes because the dragon's lair is in the high mountains, where the snow never melts entirely. Dragons can't endure heat. That's why they live in the northern mountains. Idris is far too warm for them. No one really knows why this dragon came here in the first place, or why it's stayed so many years. Though some of my father's advisers have theories. But that's why the dragon seldom raids in the summer, and why his raids on the first cold nights in autumn are so fierce. Because of his hunger, and his anger over his summer-long fast. That's why we need the map as well—not many people live around there, not anymore. We can't depend on being able to ask for directions."

"You're really going after the dragon?" Lysander asked. "But you're Prince Perryndon! You're your father's only child. His only heir. What happens to Idris if you get killed?"

"What will happen to Idris if the dragon *isn't* killed?" Perryn asked. "Besides, the prophecy doesn't say anything about me—just you, Prism, and the sword."

And why, he wondered, should that suddenly make him feel uneasy? It wasn't his fault the prophecy didn't name him, and even if it had, a scholar wouldn't do them much good in the fighting. His job was to bring them together, and that was all. But Perryn still had to push aside an absurd feeling of being left out.

"You can do it," he told Lysander firmly.

"Not me," said Lysander. "Prince or no prince, I'm not fighting the dragon. I want to live and go south."

"But you will help me get the Sword of Samhain, won't you? You did promise that much."

"Certainly." The bard grinned. "Anything you say, My Prince. We need a pick and shovel? Torches, too. It's going to be dark in that tomb."

Perryn scowled. "That was too easy. What aren't you telling me?"

"Perryn, you're not going to find the Sword of Samhain." Lysander's voice was suddenly serious. "It's the greatest weapon in the history of Idris. It was forged by Samhain the smith, in the elder days." The bard's voice grew dreamy and his eyes shone. "Half the heroes of legend used it; there are hundreds of songs about its deeds. Rhyden defeated the army of the sea people with the Sword of Samhain. It slew the giant Orok, at Lysar ford. If you had the Sword of Samhain, you probably *could* slay the dragon. A man could do anything with that sword—and all the great warriors knew it. The tomb it was buried in must have been robbed dozens of times. Even if we do find the tomb, and with your directions I suppose we might, the sword won't be there. Not that sword."

"But you'll help us look?"

"Why not? Grave robbing sounds like the safest thing you've asked me to do so far. There are several villages between here and the foothills, so I can sing for the equipment we need."

"Lysander, that may not...ah..."

"What?"

"Nothing."

IT WAS RAINING WHEN THEY REACHED THE FIRST village. Lysander wanted to go straight to an inn, but Perryn

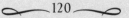

insisted he wait with Prism while Perryn checked out the town. At least the rain made it seem natural for him to pull his hood over his face.

Perryn found the public message board and gazed at the poster in horror. Someone had earned ten gold.

The Prince is believed to be traveling with a bard, a tall, thin man with light brown hair. Perryn read the rest of the poster and shuddered. They didn't have a picture of Lysander, but the description was a good one, and combined with the sketch of Perryn...

He had no choice now—he had to tell the bard. With a quick look around to be sure no one was watching, Perryn pulled down the poster and tucked it into his belt. Carefully concealing his face, he hurried out of the town.

"HAVE YOU SATISFIED YOURSELF THAT THIS VILLAGE is worthy of our humble efforts, Your Highness? May we go and get out of the rain now?" Lysander shivered elaborately.

"No, we can't," said Perryn. "You can't go into this town—at least, not carrying that harp—and I can't go in at all. We'll pass it by and find shelter in a barn or something."

The bard's jaw dropped. "But why? Perryn, what's going on?"

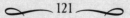

"I should have told you sooner," Perryn confessed. "Above all, a scholar respects truth. But I was ... it's difficult."

"Tell me anyway."

"I'll do better than that; I'll show you." Perryn handed the poster to the bard.

Lysander unfolded it and began to read. His eyes widened. His mouth opened and closed. Angry color flooded his cheeks.

"What does it say?" asked Prism.

"Well, you see—" Perryn began.

"Kidnapping!" the bard howled. "I'm wanted for kidnapping! Dead or alive. They'll kill me. Two hundred gold pieces. They'll stand in line to kill me!"

He threw down the poster and glared at Perryn.

"I'll tell them you're innocent," said Perryn. "It will all be cleared up. But until it is—"

"Until it is, I won't be able to show my face from one end of Idris to the other!"

"Many people could fit that description. As long as you claim to be something besides a bard—"

"How am I supposed to eat, if I can't sing without being arrested—or worse!—by every man in the room who'd like to get his hands on two hundred gold pieces? Two hundred!

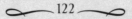

I could live very well on two hundred gold pieces myself."

Prism gasped. "Are you suggesting—"

"If you turn me in, I'll tell them you really did kidnap me," Perryn said.

Lysander scowled at him, but Perryn straightened his shoulders and met the bard's gaze squarely. It was Lysander who finally looked away.

"I didn't mean it. But blast it, Perryn. Why are you doing this? Why—"

"There's something else I need to tell you. The man who's hunting me, Cedric, the master of arms...."

LYSANDER GREW CALMER AS PERRYN TOLD HIS TALE.

"There's only one thing that makes me believe a word of that story," he said when Perryn finished.

"What?"

"You said your arms master signed that letter Cerdic."

"So?"

"Cerdic is a Norse name."

Yet another bit of information that wasn't in any of Perryn's books. After several weeks in Lysander's company, he was beginning to realize that bardic knowledge could be the equal of a library—in some ways even better.

"We haven't been in a town since we went into the forest," said Perryn. "Cedric must have lost our trail by now. Don't you think so?"

"I think that you're going to be assassinated," said the bard. "And I'm going to be executed for kidnapping. But we'll certainly avoid towns from now on. Or maybe . . ." He looked Perryn over thoughtfully. "If I don't admit I'm a bard and you change your appearance . . . it's only those spectacles that are distinctive, because so few people your age wear them. If you took them off—"

"I'd be tripping over chairs and talking to the cloak rack," Perryn told him. "They'd guess."

"All right," said Lysander. "I have a little money left. You wait here with Prism and my harp and I'll simply buy what we need." He handed his harp to Perryn and vanished, grumbling, into the rain.

"I don't wish to cast aspersions on anyone's character," said Prism softly. "But are you sure . . ."

"Yes," said Perryn. "He's a true bard." *He has to be. Otherwise, it's all been for nothing.*

LYSANDER'S MONEY WAS ENOUGH TO PURCHASE food, but no more. In the end they were forced to steal a pick, a shovel, and three torches from a farmer's shed.

"We can't even leave him something else in exchange," said Perryn regretfully. "We'll need everything we have in the mountains."

"Maybe there'll be some junk left in the tomb," Lysander consoled him. "Things that a grave robber wouldn't have bothered with hundreds of years ago might be valuable now. And we can return the tools on our way back."

Prism sniffed. "It's still very dishonest. As a unicorn, I can have nothing to do with such things."

"Nobody asked you to," the bard retorted. "There's no way you could help, except . . . maybe you could carry a torch. We could tie it to your horn."

"I will have nothing to do with stolen goods," said Prism.

"Of all the—"

"But you're helping us look for the tomb," Perryn pointed out, "even though you know we plan to . . . ah, borrow what's there."

Prism considered this carefully. "If you were not the Prince of Idris, I would probably refuse."

"Snob," the bard muttered.

The unicorn ignored him. "But since you are the direct heir of Albion, the twenty-seventh warrior-king, you have a

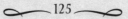

right to the tomb's contents. So I will be honored to assist Your Highness."

IT TOOK THEM TWO MORE DAYS TO REACH THE valley, and when they got there, they couldn't find the tomb.

"The directions said that the shadow of Hevyd's sword would touch the door at sunset." Perryn frowned. "It's sunset, and there is Hevyd's sword." He gestured toward the spire of rock that rose from the valley floor. Even without the map's identification, he'd have known it for what it was. The tip of its shadow darkened the ground at his feet—the flat ground of an open meadow. Not a barrow mound in sight. "So where's the tomb?"

"Maybe it's completely buried." Lysander pulled his heavy cloak closer. A few snow drifts still lingered in the foothills. With the sun's departure the night was growing cold.

"We should be able to see the top of the mound, at least."

"Maybe Hevyd's sword moved," said the bard.

"Nonsense," Perryn snapped. "It might have worn down a bit over the years, but—"

"So maybe the sun moved! Maybe the tomb moved! Maybe the directions are completely wrong. We've been searching this valley for hours and we can't find the tomb. Can we leave now?"

"If you don't have any helpful suggestions," Prism remarked. "You'd do better to—"

"Of course!" Perryn shouted. "What a fool I am! Why didn't I think of it? The sun does move!"

"What?" The others stared at him.

"It does! It's mapped on my globe of the stars. As the world moves around the sun it gets . . . never mind. Let me think a minute. It's spring now so the sun's almost at equinox. In the summer it would go that way, so the shadow would move in an arc that way. In the winter it would be the opposite. Lysander, what time of year was the twenty-seventh king buried?"

"How should I . . . wait! The song talks about ladies clad in drifting silks. They held the funeral feast outside because the crowd was too big for the hall. They couldn't do that in the snow. High summer, from the sound of it."

"Then it's this way." Perryn snatched up the shovel. "Come on!"

The tomb had been dug into the side of a hill. The entrance was within ten feet of the place where Perryn told them to start looking.

Lysander fingered the carving on the lintel, the only part of the door that showed above the ground.

"Start digging." Perryn sank his shovel into the fall of earth that blocked it.

Despite Prism's comments on the impropriety of their conduct, they made good progress. The crescent moon had barely risen when they finished.

Perryn stared at the huge stone doors in awe. "Are they sealed?"

"There's one way to find out." Lysander grabbed one of the ornate iron handles and heaved. With a resounding clank, the handle broke. Lysander fell over. Prism snickered.

"It's rusted through," said the bard, examining it. "All right, moon beam, if you're so smart you open the door."

"If you wish." Prism stepped forward delicately, inserted the tip of her horn into the narrow crack between the doors, and pried.

The door grated and the hinges squealed, but it opened. The moist air that sighed from the tomb was colder than the breeze off the snowdrifts.

"It shouldn't be this easy," said Lysander. "Light the torches."

Torch in hand, the bard stepped in and examined the

backs of the doors. "It doesn't look like these were ever sealed," he said nervously. "That's crazy."

"Maybe whatever they used to lock it was on the outside, and it rotted, or was stolen," said Perryn.

"Maybe," said the bard.

"In any case, we're in. Prism, whatever you do, don't faint. If we get into trouble, we may not have time to carry you out."

"I'll try not to," said the unicorn dubiously.

Perryn raised his torch and started down the tunnel, the stone floor uneven beneath his feet. Elaborately carved statues of the most famous ancient warriors stood at the sides of the long hall.

When the flickering torchlight first caught the man-shaped form on the floor, Perryn thought one of the statues had fallen. Then the light picked out the hollow sockets and shining teeth of the skull.

"A fellow grave robber?" The bard went forward to examine the body, and Perryn followed reluctantly. The man's flesh was entirely gone, but scraps of his boots and his heavy leather belt remained. The bard rolled the skeleton over.

Perryn shuddered. "Don't you dare faint, Prism."

"Why should I?" The unicorn sounded surprised. "It's only bones."

"Perryn." Lysander's voice was tense. "There isn't a mark here to show how this man died."

"Maybe he was shot by an arrow and it didn't hit a bone," Perryn suggested. "A falling-out among thieves?"

"Then where's the arrowhead?"

"So maybe he was stabbed," said Perryn impatiently. Part of him was curious, but the sword was so close! The thought of claiming the final piece of the prophecy made his heart beat faster. "Come on. There's nothing we can do for him." Perryn strode down the corridor. The torchlight found another skeleton. And another.

"This is worse than Wyr forest," said the bard. "Why do I let you talk me into these things?"

A muted gasp in Perryn's mind warned him.

"Prism!" The unicorn's eyes were rolling up. "Take deep breaths and put your head down. Another breath. Another. That's it."

The unicorn's eyes came back to normal, and she looked frantically at the dim corridor. With a mind-splitting shriek she bolted out of the tomb.

Perryn winced. "At least she didn't faint."

The bard was rubbing his temples. "Was that supposed to be an improvement?" Then Lysander jumped and stared wildly around him.

"What is it?"

"Something touched me." The bard's face was pale.

"But there's nothing here!" Something cold brushed across Perryn's face and he flinched. "What was that?"

The cold touch ran over his arm next.

Lysander backed up against the wall, his eyes searching the shadows. "Perryn, we've got to get out of here." He started forward and then jumped back.

A freezing hand ran over Perryn's shoulder and down the inside of his arm. He yelped and swung his torch. The cold vanished.

"Use the torch," he yelled.

The bard burst away from the wall. Swinging his torch wildly he ran for the exit.

Perryn followed. The icy air was thick in front of him, yielding only to the flame. Frigid hands stroked his back as he ran, only stopping as he burst through the door and out into the night. The cold, fresh air felt warm on his chilled skin. He was gasping with fear, and felt deeply, strangely weary. He stared at the open door of the tomb.

There was nothing there.

"Ghosts." Prism came to stand beside him. She was trembling all over, her eyes fixed on the doorway. "They're going back now. They probably can't leave the corridor."

"You can see them?" Perryn asked.

"You mean you can't?"

"Well, now we know why they didn't need to lock the door." Lysander joined them. "And what happened to those men in there."

"The ghosts killed them? But how?" Perryn asked. "And why?" Ghost stories were one of the few subjects that hadn't interested him, and now he regretted it.

"For the warmth," Prism told him. "For the life in their bodies. Ghosts are greedy for it. They suck it right out of you."

"How do you know?"

"I could hear them talking about it. They're the ghosts of King Albion's enemies. They don't have a choice." She looked down, refusing to meet Perryn's eyes, and he decided he didn't want to know what else the ghosts had said. The ancient mages had possessed great power, but not even the legends claimed that they were all good men. Some of them emphatically weren't. Perhaps the loss of man-made magic in the world wasn't such a bad thing after all.

"That's that," said the bard. "No Sword of Samhain for us. It'll be nice and warm in the south this time of year."

"No!" said Perryn. "I won't turn back. The sword is in there and I'm going to get it."

"The sword may be there," said Lysander. "I can't imagine a grave robber who could get through that. So how, may I ask, do you plan to do it?"

"With fire," said Perryn. "They gave way before our torches. We fought our way out with them. We can fight our way in."

"I knew I should have turned you in for the reward," said Lysander. "I am never going in there again."

"I am," said Perryn. "Before I lose my nerve."

He grasped his torch firmly and ran through the mouth of the tomb.

"Wait! Perryn, stop!" the bard cried.

Then he was through the door. The cold swirled around him as he thrust forward, spinning and slashing wildly with his torch. He could almost see them, like wisps of mist at the edges of his vision, but when he looked for them they vanished. His back was growing cold. He couldn't defend it and still move forward.

Perryn kept going. Icy hands stroked his spine. His head ached from the chill, and his back was freezing.

With a flurry of footsteps and a roar of fire, Lysander appeared behind him. Back to back, they moved slowly down the long corridor. A few frigid hands reached past their whirling torches, but not many.

A dark doorway loomed and they stepped through it together. The swirling cold of the ghosts vanished.

"We made it!" Perryn slid to the floor; his knees were limp.

"No thanks to you," Lysander declared furiously. "What were you doing rushing in like that without a word of warning? You could have been killed. *I* could have been killed!"

"What was there to wait for?"

"For one thing," said Lysander, "we could have kindled the third torch."

"Oh." Perryn blushed.

Lysander could have been killed, but he'd followed Perryn anyway. The warmth of that knowledge banished the last of the chill from Perryn's heart. It had been a long time since he'd had a friend. Or was this the first time? For years he'd wished for a friend—and now that he'd found one, Perryn had led him straight into danger, and would probably lead him into more. He pushed the thought aside. "At least we made it." Perryn lifted his torch to look around him and gasped.

The tomb of Albion, twenty-seventh of the great warrior-kings of Idris, held all the things he had most cherished in his life. A game board caught Perryn's eye; the playing pieces were hounds and hares, cast in silver and gold, the silver black with tarnish. The board was inlaid with emeralds. Clearly, the ghosts had been good guardians. Perryn and Lysander must be the first people to see this room since the doors were closed. The rusty suit of armor beside the game board was plain steel, but beautifully crafted. It was also dented and worn. The king's armor. Not ceremonial armor, but the armor he had fought in.

Perryn staggered to his feet and went to the coffin in the center of the room. It was stone, the lid carved into a likeness of King Albion. He was shorter than Perryn had expected, and bore no resemblance to either Perryn or his father. On his chest, its hilt slipped between his stone hands, lay a sword. It was very plain, but its grace and strength showed through the rust that covered it.

"The Sword of Samhain," Lysander breathed. He hadn't even glanced at the other treasures around them. "The sword with which King Darian slew the evil wizard Andross. The sword that defeated the army of Mandeen the soul slayer."

Perryn reached out. Grasping the sword, he worked it loose from the carved king's stone fingers. It slid free in a shower of rust.

"Adan, the second warrior-king, was knighted with that sword," Lysander murmured reverently.

"And what a party that was!" The sword vibrated in Perryn's hands as the voice vibrated in his mind. He almost dropped it. "All the lords and half the ladies were drunk and a walloping brawl started. Old Duran—he was the first king, though they just called 'em barons back then— he should have stopped it, but he was under the table by that time and Adan himself was in the thick of things. It was almost as much fun as a battle. Who're you fellers?"

Lysander's mouth was hanging open, but Perryn wasn't as surprised. He remembered reading that the Sword of Samhain had a mind-voice—like the Mirror of Idris once had. Though he *hadn't* expected it to be quite so ... alive.

"I'm Perryn. I mean, Prince Perryndon, son of Rovan, the forty-fourth warrior-king of Idris. My companion is the bard Lysander."

"Forty-fourth king? How long have I been moldering in this boring box? I'm the Sword of Samhain, which means I was forged by Samhain, way back in the elder days. He was a pretty good smith and a pretty good wizard, but he'd have been a total loss as a fighter if he hadn't had me. I'm pleased to death to meet you, so to speak. Call me Sam. And tell me why I've been sitting around here getting rusty for seventeen generations. Albion's kid swore he'd have me out of here within the week!"

"He probably tried," said Perryn, "But I think the ghosts stopped him."

"Ghosts? You mean old Alby brought in ghosts to guard me? No wonder it's been so long. Never could abide ghosts—horrid, chilly things." A grating chuckle sounded in Perryn's mind. "'Course, they can't abide me either. It's one of my powers, dispelling ghosts. But tell me, what brought you fellers this way?"

"A prophecy," said Perryn. There was no use in concealing anything from the sword. This was a time for truth. "A prophecy made by Mardon the magus, that the Sword of Samhain, a true bard, and a unicorn could slay a dragon. I have the other two, but we need you. Will you do it?"

"Mardon's prophecy? But he only made ... wait a minute.

You mean a dragon's turned up? A real one? You want to take me dragon slaying?"

"Yes." Perryn held his breath. It might be possible to find another bard, or another unicorn, somewhere, but if the sword refused . . .

"Hot fights and hotter women! A battle! After all these years. Let me at 'em!" roared the sword.

But Prince Perryndon's enemies
sought to stop the prophecy.

10

"THEN THERE WAS THE TIME ME AND OLD BRYNDON took on the snake woman of the vanishing caves," the sword's voice grated.

"Half-python, half-woman, and all evil. Her hair was a mass of poisonous vipers," the bard chanted.

"Naw, she wasn't a monster herself. She just had a pack of trained snakes, or maybe she controlled 'em by magic. Never found out. Anyway, she had this big old python, twenty feet if it was an inch, and he ambushed us just before we reached the main chamber of the cave. There we were . . ."

"Humph," Prism sniffed. As a creature of magic herself, she was notably unimpressed by Sam. Especially when she discovered that she had to carry the armor.

Sam had insisted they remove Albion's armor and war ax from the tomb.

"It's not magical or anything," he told them. "But I've gotten kind of used to working with folks in armor. I'd feel downright nekked if someone weren't wearing it. And the ax, well, I've been talking to it for the last couple of centuries. 'Course it didn't talk back, but I got fond of it. Kind of like a pet, you know?"

So now Prism carried a pack with the armor, and when she complained, Lysander told her to be grateful she was too small for anyone to ride. The bard had accepted the heavy war ax without complaint, and now Perryn watched him uneasily, as he sat by the campfire listening to Sam. Perryn wasn't certain why he was so worried. He had assembled everyone he needed to make the prophecy come true. Even his father would have to acknowledge that. He should be rejoicing! *And yet...*

When the cannons were gone, when their king, half-mad with grief, was rocking his wife's broken body in his arms, the king's men had tried to fight the dragon in the old way, with spears, arrows, and swords. They must have injured the beast—the fever known as the dragon's wrath, which only occurred when a dragon's blood touched the blood of a man, had killed almost all of his father's wounded within a day. So the dragon could be cut by normal weapons, and magical weapons should work much better. Still, only a quarter of the men who had set out with their king had returned alive.

"... Eighty of 'em there was, and me and Jadon with only fifteen men," Sam continued.

Prism sniffed again.

"But the song says Mandeen's army was hundreds strong," the bard protested. "And you and Jadon were alone."

"You got to watch out for them songs, young feller. Never did know a bard that could resist adding a little polish to the truth. Not that some of 'em aren't grand fighters, as well as grand musicians, but they do exaggerate. Nope, there was eighty of them, and seventeen of us, and the battlefield a sea of mud. It had been raining all week, you see, and—"

"Lysander," said Perryn. "Can I talk to you? Alone?"

"Perryn, you interrupted—"

"Don't worry about that," Sam said. "I know I'm talking too much. Always did, and after all that time with no one to listen, I'll probably rattle on forever if you let me. You go talk to the prince. If we're gonna fight a dragon there's plans to make, yes siree. Plans to make and . . ."

Perryn dragged the bard away from the fire, out of the range of the sword's mind-voice, which seemed to carry about as far as a normal voice would. Perryn hoped the same was true of the sword's hearing.

"Perryn, if you're going to make battle plans I'd think you'd want Sam's help. He has far more experience than we do. More than you can imagine."

"Battle plans? Lysander, are you actually considering fighting the dragon?"

"Yes!" said the bard enthusiastically. "Think of it! A new legend of the Sword of Samhain, in our own time! With that song in my repertoire I'll be one of the great bards of history. Not to mention the richest. *And* how the tale of my exploits will affect the ladies! I'll start on the melody line as soon as—"

"Forget Sam; what about you? Do you even know how to fight?"

"Well, it's not like the old days, when most bards were warriors, too, but a wandering bard has to know how to fight. . . ." Lysander paused. "At least a bit. And the Sword of Samhain will make up for any deficiencies on my part."

"But you never believed in the prophecy! I can tell that

meeting Sam has impressed you, and the last thing I want is to discourage you, but my father took two cannons and fifty knights out to slay that beast and only a handful survived. I know Sam was a legendary fighter, but—"

"You don't understand, Perryn. You think Sam is bragging, but he isn't. In fact, he's being modest. If anything can slay that dragon, the Sword of Samhain can."

"But he's rusting to bits!"

"What's the matter with you, Perryn? The prophecy is coming true! What's the problem? Don't you think Sam can do it?"

"I'm not sure," said Perryn. "I'm just not sure."

"Then ask him yourself," said the bard. "I'm going back to the fire—it's cold out here."

"THERE WE WERE," THE SWORD WAS TELLING THE bored unicorn when they returned. "All but five of us down and twenty of them still to go. 'At least we've reduced the odds,' Jadon says. I—"

"Sam," said Perryn sinking down beside the sword. "I'd like to ask you a few things."

"Certainly! Glad to help out. What do you want to know?"

"Ah ... have you ever killed a dragon before?"

"Nope, never have," the sword answered cheerfully. "It'll be a real challenge, facing something new at my age."

"Then you don't know how to go about it? At all?"

"I never was much for all those tactical flourishes. Just hit what I'm swung at, that's what I do best."

"But are you sure you can? I mean, at your age?"

"Well, I may have lost a bit of the old edge, sitting around in the damp all that time. Damp gets into steel, you know? Give us a lick with the whetstone, boy. That'll do her."

Perryn took the sword into his hands. Flakes of rust peeled off against his fingers. The sword's edges seemed to be entirely rotted away.

"I don't think I'd better," he said nervously.

"Ah, save all me metal for the dragon. Good idea."

"But what are we to do?" asked Perryn. "How do we start?"

"I can't say for sure. But when you don't really know what you're up against, my favorite thing is to charge straight in and fight for all you're worth!"

"But if you don't know what you're up against—"

"That way you find out real fast," said the sword. "I remember once..."

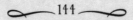

IT WAS HARD TO GET AWAY FROM THE OTHERS, TO be alone with the mirror. But the longer he watched Lysander, Sam, and Prism together, the more Perryn worried. Finally he excused himself. At least the night was cold enough that no one wondered why he extracted his cloak from his satchel before leaving the fire, and he managed to conceal the mirror in its folds.

"Mirror of Idris," he said softly, settling cross-legged in the grass. "It's Perryn. Can you show me . . . ?" He intended to ask whether these unlikely heroes could succeed in killing the dragon, but the usual question rose to his lips instead. "Can you show me my father's reaction to my flight?"

The mirror swirled just once and then the image formed—a battle against the Norse. It was day in the meadow between the rolling hills, and enemy warriors swarmed down the slopes toward his father's men. Perryn watched with fear and pride as the king rallied his troops against charge after charge until the Norsemen finally retreated.

Perryn frowned. Why hadn't his father used those hills himself? Safranos of Nardon wrote that if there was a hill or a valley within fifty leagues of a battlefield, a wise commander would make use of it. His father probably had his reasons, but—

The mirror's focus tightened on the king. "We're losing too many men," King Rovan told the officer who stood beside him, watching the wounded carried off to the surgeons. "We didn't get enough recruits this winter—and having to send almost a hundred soldiers after that worthless boy didn't help."

The officer looked shocked. "But Highness, no one begrudges the men sent to look for the prince! Your son's safety has to come first."

The king grunted. There was nothing on his face but concern for the next battle they'd have to fight.

This was the reaction he'd been trying to see for so long? His father's love. . . .

"Isn't anyone worried about me?" Perryn whispered.

A new image flashed to the mirror's surface. The palace housekeeper, making up his bed with her own hands though that task was far beneath her dignity. Her face was tight with distress. A groom currying Perryn's favorite mare with more than ordinary care. One servant after another, their faces flashing over the glass, faster and faster.

The ones who cared. The only ones who cared.

Perryn laid the mirror on the grass and wept.

"WHERE ON EARTH WERE YOU?" LYSANDER demanded the moment Perryn appeared. It had taken Perryn some time to compose himself before he returned to the camp. He prayed his reddened eyes and nose would be invisible in the firelight.

"We were about to send out a search party," the bard went on. "Are you feeling all right? What's wrong?"

Prism was silent but her ears were pricked toward Perryn, her eyes dark with concern. Perhaps there were a few who cared besides the servants.

"It doesn't matter," said Perryn, as the lump in his throat eased a little. "I was just . . ." He hesitated, but there was no longer any reason to conceal it. "I was consulting the Mirror of Idris."

"The Mirror?" Lysander's brows shot up. "I thought the mirror failed after the queen . . . ah . . ."

Sam snorted. "Cheap piece of flimflam never did work right if you ask me. If it showed you something that got you upset, you should just ignore it."

"No," said Perryn wearily. "It may not show you what

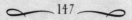

you ask for—not even what you need to see, always—but it shows the truth."

"May I see it?" Lysander asked softly. When Perryn handed it over, the bard's expression held an awed respect as well as curiosity. "So, this is the mirror of legend. How does it work?"

"You just speak to it," said Perryn. "You ask for what you want to see."

"Hmm. Mirror, show me that pretty tavern wench from Williten."

Perryn had to laugh. "It only works for the kings of Idris. Here, let me ..."

He took the mirror from Lysander's hands. "Mirror of Idris..." his voice faded as the vision formed.

"What is it?" Lysander asked.

"It's the tavern maid from Williten." If the mirror thought he needed to see her, Perryn didn't want to know why. Heat rose into his cheeks. "I think she's about to take a bath."

"What? Let me see!"

But the mirror went dark as Lysander snatched it from Perryn's hands.

"I told you it wouldn't work for you," said Perryn, grateful that particular image was gone.

"Spying on people that way is most improper," Prism added.

"Well, if you're all going to be so prim about it," said Lysander. "Can you show me how it works?"

Perryn shrugged. "Mirror of Idris, show me the way to the dragon's lair."

This time the image formed almost at once.

"It's a road," said the bard, looking over Perryn's shoulder. "A fork in the road. Is that the way to the dragon's lair?"

"I don't think so," said Perryn, frowning at the familiar scene. "The mirror has showed me this place several times before. It probably doesn't mean anything at all. The mirror's pretty erratic these days."

"If the mirror showed this to you several times, perhaps it's something you need to see," Prism suggested.

"An empty road?"

"A fork in the road," said the bard, still gazing into the mirror with fascinated eyes. "Maybe it's a metaphor—it's trying to show you that you'll have to make some sort of choice."

"It doesn't work that way," said Perryn. "At least, it never

has before. It shows the kings of Idris what they *need* to see. Directly. No metaphors."

And my choice is already made. If he couldn't win his father's love, he had to earn his respect. Or he really would be worthless.

"We'd better go to bed now. We should get an early start in the morning," said Perryn.

The image of the empty roads lingered in the mirror, its light glowing through the seams of Perryn's satchel for quite some time.

THEY SET OFF AT A BRISK PACE NEXT MORNING. Lysander carried Sam, listening to his stories eagerly, adding stanzas from ballads whenever the sword paused. He almost bumped into Perryn before he noticed the prince had stopped.

"What is it?" The bard looked at the narrow gorge that followed the stream into the mountains. "Wait a minute. Isn't this the place . . . ?"

"Yes," said Perryn. "This is the place the mirror was showing me." Apprehension shivered through his nerves. But why? The mirror had only revealed a place he was destined to find.

"Then it was truly guiding you all along," said the bard. "Leading you here. What is this road, anyway?"

"According to the notes on the map, it used to be the Udo Valley Road," Perryn told him. "But now they call it Dragon's Gap. This road leads straight to the dragon's valley. I've never been in this area before. I didn't know what it looked like."

"That's right, Prince Perryndon."

The bushes beside them crackled, and Perryn jumped. A familiar shriek made him wince. A skitter of small hooves, a flash of white, and Prism was gone.

"What was that?" asked a voice from behind them. Perryn spun, looking for a place to run, but it was too late. Four horsemen were emerging from the brush beside the road—clad in the tabards of his father's guard.

"It looked like a unicorn!" one of them said. "I didn't think they existed any more."

"That doesn't matter," said the leader. "Prince Perryndon, your father wants to see you. You and your companion are to come with us."

"But . . . wait a minute," said Lysander. "That wasn't the deal. He said I could go as soon as I had my money."

"Who said?" asked the leader.

"Why Cedric, the master of arms. Your commander. We agreed that if I brought Prince Perryndon here he'd pay me two hundred gold pieces, and then I could leave."

"No!" Perryn cried.

The guardsmen ignored him.

Lysander ignored him as well. Perryn's heart pounded sickly. *The bard had to be lying...didn't he?*

"Do you mean to tell me the money isn't here?" Lysander went on. "Of all the idiotic, incompetent—"

"If Master Cedric told you to bring the prince here, why does he have men guarding every road that leads into the mountains?" demanded the leader.

"How should I know?" Lysander shrugged. "All I know is that my money was supposed to...hmm. How long since you last received orders?"

"Four days," said the leader, staring at Lysander suspiciously.

"Then that explains part of it," said Lysander. "I only met with Cedric two days ago. Your comrades have probably been recalled. Since you were already here, he didn't need to send anyone to get the prince. What I don't understand is why he didn't send someone with my gold."

"Perhaps there wasn't time," said the leader. He looked as

if he wasn't certain whether to believe the bard's story or not. Perryn couldn't blame him for that—he wasn't certain either. "You'd better come with us."

"He had two days," Lysander complained. "If I had time to bring the prince, surely he could have sent the money."

"Then you'll accompany us back to camp," the leader said firmly.

"I'm certainly going with you," Lysander announced. "I'm not letting that boy out of my sight until the gold is in my hands. There've been too many slipups already. I assume you have a horse for me?"

THEY BOUND PERRYN'S HANDS, AND THE LEADER tied the halter of the horse Perryn rode to the cantle of his own saddle. The guardsmen had never liked him, but they wouldn't dare to bind their prince without orders. Cedric must be very sure of his influence over the king.

Perryn rode in silence. Lysander was right, the mirror had spoken true, trying to warn him about the ambush. Ambush and treachery. But since it didn't have enough power to show the future anymore, it had only been able to show the place where his plans would fail. Perhaps the prophecy was doomed to fail from the start, in his scholarly hands. Worthless, just as his father said. But it wasn't his will or courage that had failed.

When could Lysander have met with Cedric? He'd hardly been out of Perryn's sight in the last two days. Could he have slipped out of the camp at night without waking them?

His heart cried out that Lysander was a friend who wouldn't, *couldn't* betray him. But he had to admit that the bard wasn't always honest. And he had told Perryn repeatedly that he wouldn't fight the dragon. What better way to escape the prophecy than this?

Lysander chatted with the rear guard as they rode. They joked about his rusty sword, and Lysander explained that it had an old and noble history. And since he was a bard, not a swordsman, the state of the blade didn't matter to him.

Sam never uttered a word.

It was dusk when Lysander pulled his horse to a stop and dismounted. He did it so casually the others rode on for almost ten feet before they noticed and reined in their horses.

Lysander lifted his horse's hoof.

"What is it?" the leader called back.

"She started to limp. Picked up a stone, I think. It'll only take a moment." He looked quickly at Perryn, for the first time since their capture, then glanced aside.

Perryn turned to the leader, his heart pounding with sudden hope. "Do you know that Cedric plans to kill me?" he asked. "Or are you just his dupe?"

The leader snorted. "I know he gives you a hard time, lad—Your Highness, but he's not going to kill you. If you practiced a little more—"

"I don't mean fighting," said Perryn. "He's going to murder me, and make it look like an accident, because I learned that he's really a Norse spy."

The leader smiled at him. "Of course he is. But may I ask why Cedric would do such a thing? The barbarians are dirt poor. They probably couldn't scratch together a bribe big enough to tempt me, much less someone who's getting a master of arms' salary."

"It isn't the money," said Perryn. "He's one of them. His real name is Cerdic, Cerdic of the Red Bear. I saw him sign a letter that way."

"But Cedric's folks were poor farmers," said the leader. "And he can't read or write. Which means that Your Highness must be mistaken. Especially since the barbarians can't read or write either, so even if he was a Norse spy,

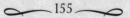

writing to another Norseman would be senseless. Besides, he's been your father's master of arms for eight years, and he was master of arms for Lord Avern for six or seven years before that, so—"

A yell from one of the rear guards interrupted him. Lysander's horse stood placidly in the road. The bard was gone.

THEY SEARCHED FOR LYSANDER FOR HALF AN HOUR and found no trace of him.

Perryn said nothing, but even the rough ropes that scraped his wrists couldn't dim his joyous relief. *A true bard.* He should never have believed those lies, not for a moment. Though Lysander would probably consider Perryn's doubts a compliment to his performance.

After that, they rode in grim silence, and Perryn didn't try to break it. These men were loyal to Cedric; they wouldn't question his lies. In the ten years since the queen's death, since the king had begun to let the reins of governance slip from his grasp, the master of arms had become powerful.

Was he more powerful than Perryn's father? Perhaps not, but the guards respected Cedric more than they did the

king—certainly more than any of them respected Perryn. Nothing he said would be believed.

Night had fallen by the time they reached the main camp. The tents set up around the big fires would hold more than fifty guardsmen, and Perryn's heart sank. He'd been hoping for a rescue after the bard escaped, but Lysander and Sam couldn't possibly get him out of this.

They rode straight for the largest tent and the leader dismounted and went in. When he came out, Cedric was with him.

"Congratulations, Harl. You've won two hundred gold for yourself and your men."

"I'm sorry about that blasted bard," said the leader. "They tricked us, that's the plain truth."

"It doesn't matter. It's the prince who's important. Cut him loose. He's not going to run anymore."

They freed Perryn's hands and helped him down. He staggered, and Cedric grasped his collar. It probably looked like Cedric was helping him stand, but the grip was like iron.

"Walk with me, Your Highness. You need to work the kinks out of your legs and I have a message to give you . . . from your father."

The guards exchanged amused glances. They thought Cedric had been told to thrash him. For a moment, fooled by the easy tone of Cedric's voice, so did Perryn. Then the truth struck him—he was going to be murdered!

He drew a breath to cry out but Cedric twisted his fist in Perryn's tunic. He couldn't breathe. He couldn't make a sound. He clawed at the noose of cloth around his throat. His feet were moving, stumbling. Bright spots formed before his eyes. His legs weakened. Just as his mind began to slide into darkness, the grip on his collar relaxed.

Perryn gasped and would have fallen if Cedric hadn't grabbed his shoulder.

They kept moving. When Perryn regained enough of his senses to look around, they were walking through a thick glade. He could no longer see the camp. If he screamed, the guardsmen would assume he was being punished. Perryn bit his lip, took a deep breath, and spoke quietly.

"It won't do you any good to kill me. I've brought them all together, and they're the ones who are going to slay the dragon. Killing me won't stop the prophecy."

"Do you think so? I don't know about this unicorn the

men claimed to see, or the rusty sword, but I've heard about your bard in the towns where we've traced you and I'm surprised you got him this far. My guess is that when you're gone he'll take the quickest road out of Idris and stay out. I'm curious though, how did you know about me? Harl told me what you said."

Cedric's voice was casual, but Perryn's thoughts raced. If he told Cedric he had learned of his identity from someone else . . . then Cedric would kill them, too.

"I saw a letter you were writing to your chieftain," he confessed. "I was using the Mirror of Idris to—"

"The Mirror," Cedric breathed. "So that was it. I've wondered where it was."

Time. He had to stall for time. If he could keep Cedric talking, maybe he could find some way to escape.

"Can I ask you . . . ah . . . how did you learn to write? I thought the Norsemen—"

"I learned to write in prison." Cedric's voice held a bitterness Perryn had never heard from him before. "We have a custom among my people, that a boy should meet his enemies before he grows his beard. As a youth, I disguised myself as one of your peasants and went into a town, explaining my accent by saying I was from a distant village. Your people are easy to fool, Prince Perryndon." A cold smile lingered on his face. "Then a drunk stumbled into me. He was rude and insulting, so I drew my dagger and avenged my honor as a warrior should. But your people don't understand honor."

Perryn tripped over a root as Cedric dragged him through a stand of thick trees, the branches lashing Perryn's face. Didn't Cedric care if there were scratches when his body was found? How was he going to explain Perryn's death? But the arms master went on speaking.

"My youth kept me from hanging, but I grew my first beard in a prison cell, five feet by five feet. I had never been confined before. I almost . . . The man in the cell across from me was learned. I lost my accent in three years of speaking to him, and he taught me to read and write—the secret your people keep so jealously to themselves."

"We don't—"

"One day Lord Avern's garrison master came to the prison to gather recruits, and I went with him." He gazed at Perryn, his eyes full of malice. "I could have escaped then, but I'd already learned one of your secrets and I wanted more."

The trees around them were thinning, admitting some light from the waning moon. Struggling against Cedric's strength was futile, but Perryn's feet seemed to have a mind of their own, skidding in the soft soil as he tried to slow their headlong pace.

"When I had leave, I secretly visited my people," Cedric continued, hauling Perryn easily beside him despite his resistance. "Over the years, I shared my new knowledge with them. My chieftain reads and writes as well as I do now. And knowing your fighting methods has helped us to defeat you more than a hundred warriors would. But most of all," he smiled again, enjoying his boasting, "it has helped to know the king's plans."

"You won't get away with it." Perryn's voice shook. "My father will—"

"Your father is a drunk, and the death of his heir . . ." Cedric pushed him through the last of the trees. They stood near the top of a high cliff, only a dozen feet from the edge. "It will probably finish him."

"You can't." Perryn's mouth was dry.

"A tragic accident," said Cedric. "You were running to escape your punishment and in your panic, in the dark, you didn't see the cliff. I tried to warn you, but—"

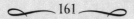

"No!" Perryn shouted. "Please, Cedric, no. I beg you!" He threw his arms around Cedric's waist.

Cedric cursed and shoved him off. Perryn stumbled several feet closer to the cliff, but when he straightened, he held Cedric's dagger in his fist.

Cedric began to laugh. Then he stopped. "What? No tears? By the old gods, you might have made a man after all. What a pity." He lunged at Perryn, who jumped away, and they began to circle.

The pattern of attack and retreat was as familiar as an old nightmare. Perryn tried to tell himself that this time the master of arms wore no padding and carried no weapon. And Perryn had his glasses on. He had a chance!

Twice Perryn slashed at Cedric, but Cedric leaped nimbly aside and continued to press him back. The trees were many feet behind the master of arms now. Perryn realized he must be almost at the edge of the cliff and glanced behind.

Cedric sprang. His hand closed around Perryn's wrist and twisted. Perryn yelped with pain, and the dagger clattered on the stones.

"Now," said Cedric, stepping closer to the cliff. Perryn struggled with all his strength. Cedric took another step.

A cry of rage echoed in Perryn's mind. Prism ran toward them along the cliff edge, her white body gleaming in the dark. The spiral horn was lowered like a lance as she charged, straight at Cedric.

"What in the—" Cedric let go of Perryn, who fell to his knees. The master of arms snatched up the dagger, moonlight glinting on its blade.

Prism stopped a few feet from him. Perryn could see her legs wobbling with terror—he would have sworn she was about to faint, but she braced herself in place, lifting her head in silent challenge, holding Cedric's attention until Sam's point touched his back.

"Don't move," said Lysander. "Or I'll run you through."

"Turn around," grated Sam. "Turn around and fight like a man."

"Don't listen to him," said Lysander, pressing Sam's point harder against Cedric's spine. "I'm the one holding the sword. Tie him up, Perryn. There's some rope in Prism's pack."

Sam complained bitterly as Perryn bound the master of arms with trembling hands. "I can't just skewer someone tied up like a chicken. My honor counts for something, even if he hasn't got any."

"Gag the man too," Lysander ordered. "We don't want him yelling for help. We've got enough to worry about."

Cedric didn't appear to be inclined to yell, or try much of anything. The Norse believed in magic. The sight of Prism had stunned him. Hearing Sam's mind-voice had left him still and silent, though Sam's blade lying across his throat might have had something to do with that.

"Why should we be worried?" asked Prism. "We've saved Perryn! I saw what that man was going to do." She shuddered. "It was horrible."

"You were very brave." Perryn stroked her neck. "All of you were."

"Prism was brave," said Lysander. "I was clever. I'm the one who devised this bit of distraction and ambush. And on very short notice, I might add."

"How?" Perryn wrapped his arms around his knees and tried to stop shaking. Then it occurred to him that Cedric had almost killed him—he had a right to shake!

Lysander put Sam down and went to check the knots that bound the master of arms.

"We've been following you all afternoon," he said. "Prism caught up with Sam and me when we got away, but we didn't have a chance to get at you until Cedric hauled you off alone. Then we had to think fast." He nodded at the bound master of arms. "I must say, I think it worked rather neatly. There's only one problem left."

"What's that?" Perryn asked.

"What do we do with him?"

"Cut him loose, give him a sword, and let Perryn and me at 'em," demanded Sam. "I'll carve out the coward's gizzard! Trying to push the boy off a cliff!"

"I hate blood," said Prism.

"We can't just leave him," said Lysander. "Even tied up. Sooner or later he'd work himself loose, or his men would find him, and then we'd have the whole troop on our heels."

"We can't leave him," Perryn agreed. "And I can't kill him, either. I'm sorry, Sam, but I just learned something about myself. I always thought that if a fight was really important, somehow I'd be able to do it. But my father was right about that . . . about me." For a moment the pain of acknowledging it overwhelmed him—but a scholar faced the truth. He steadied his voice and went on. "I'm not a fighter. I'm not a fighter and I never will be. I can't kill him."

After a moment of silence Sam said softly, "A fighter isn't

necessarily someone who swings a sword. It's someone who goes into a bad place and comes out on his own two feet. Or maybe he doesn't come out, but the bad place ain't so bad anymore. Anyway, it always seemed to me that the best fighters were those who went with their strengths. Whether it was swinging a sword or not."

"After all," said Lysander, "you brought together the prophecy. Compared to that, thinking up a way to keep this spy out from under our feet should be easy."

"Actually, it is easy." Perryn managed a smile. "I may not be able to kill him, but if he sleeps for the next three weeks it won't matter who finds him. His men won't act without orders; they'll just take him home. Where's that book on the black-bog waters? I have to figure out the dosage."

"What usually happens to captured traitors?" asked Prism.

"I'm not sure." Perryn dug into the pack the bard held out to him. "No one's been convicted of treason since Olin Blackhand, and that was four hundred years ago."

"What happened to him?"

Perryn's hands stilled. "Even my father wouldn't do that. He couldn't."

"Really?" said Lysander. "I wouldn't bet money on it. Anyway, that's not our problem. All we have to worry about is the dragon. Right?"

"Right," said Perryn weakly.

And so they went to fight the dragon —
the bard, the unicorn, and the sword.
Just as the prophecy had foretold.

11

AFTER THEY PASSED THROUGH THE DRAGON'S GAP, THEY climbed for two days. Snow lay all around them.

"Be quiet," snapped Perryn in a whisper, for the fourth time.

"I am quiet," the bard whispered back. "Sam's the one who's talking. You said we won't reach the dragon's lair till evening. And the dragon's nocturnal. You think it can hear us in its sleep, at this distance?"

"It's not the dragon I'm worried about. It's *that*." Perryn pointed at the hillside above them.

"What?" asked the bard. "There's nothing up there but snow.

"Shh!" Perryn hissed. "There's too much snow up there and your voice might bring it down. Any voice might."

"Sam's and Prism's won't," the bard said. His voice softened even further. "It was an avalanche that killed your mother, wasn't it?"

"It was about this time of year." Perryn's throat was tight. He barely remembered her, but her death had begun the changes in his life. The change in his father. "Early spring is the worst time for avalanches, but they didn't know that. The dragon's raids had been fierce that winter and my father had been making plans for months. He forbade my mother to come, but she wanted to see the dragon slain. To be near my father, I guess. She disguised herself as a powder boy and bribed the gunners to take her with them. They set the cannons under a huge bank of snow. It was the best place for them to hit the dragon, and they were so ignorant. The noise of the first shot brought it all down."

His father had blamed himself. He hadn't known about the danger of the avalanche. No one could have known back then. *I was in command,* he'd cried out once, in drunken anguish, when Perryn was six: *I should have seen the threat, should have known she was there, should have known . . .*

No wonder the king drank so deeply in the spring.

"You know a lot about it," the bard commented.

"Studying avalanches is what taught me to be a scholar. In the beginning I just wanted to find out how my mother died, but then I got interested. I read everything I could find and talked to people in the high villages. I wrote a paper about how you can set off an avalanche deliberately, when no one's in its path, so it won't fall unexpectedly. I sent the paper to all the mountain villages. My tutor even sent it to the universities. Some of the villages wrote back to say they'd used my idea, that it would save many lives."

"What did the universities say?"

"They said it was good research." Perryn shrugged. "I was only nine."

"Is that when you ran away?"

Perryn nodded bitterly. "I'd barely reached the next village before the guardsmen brought me back."

His father hadn't bothered to look for Perryn then, either. Why had Perryn thought it would be different now? Just because he'd gotten farther this time? Been gone for weeks, instead of two days?

"That's pretty impressive scholarship, for a nine-year-old." The bard's voice was growing louder.

"Shh!" said Perryn.

BY SUNSET THEY HAD REACHED THE ENTRANCE OF THE valley where the dragon laired.

"According to what the survivors said, there should be a cave in that cliff." Perryn gestured. "They stored their powder there to keep it dry. We can camp in it tonight and ... and face the dragon when it returns in the morning. It should be tired after a night of hunting."

The bard's cheeks were red with cold; he looked about eagerly. "A fit setting for a new legend."

"What am I going to eat?" Prism was almost invisible against the snow, except for the pack of armor she still carried.

"Paw through the surface," Perryn suggested. "There's probably grass beneath it."

Prism muttered something Perryn was glad he couldn't hear and shook herself free of the pack.

Lysander leaped forward and caught it. "That's right, drop a sack of tin cans down the rocks. We wouldn't want to surprise the dragon tomorrow, would we?"

"Ah, about that armor," Sam began.

Lysander sat the pack down gently. It was growing lighter again. They only had enough food for about four days. "Yes?"

"You might want to try getting into it while it's still light. It may need a few adjustments."

THE TWENTY-SEVENTH WARRIOR-KING OF IDRIS had been six inches shorter than Lysander.

"Not a chance," the bard finally conceded. "None of it fits. And we're out of light." He scowled at Perryn. There were several kegs of old gunpowder in the cave, and Perryn wouldn't let him light the torch.

"I can't fight without someone in armor around me," Sam fretted. "It just won't seem right."

"I know," said Lysander. "Prism can carry it. We'll buckle it together, set it on her back, and the dragon will think there's two of us. In fact, since it will look more formidable, the dragon will probably go for her first. Then we can ... don't faint, Prism. Isn't courage part of the unicorn creed?"

"You said I wouldn't have to do anything dangerous! You promised!"

"You don't have to," Lysander said quickly. "But danger alone won't darken you, will it? And think how much the other unicorns will respect you when they hear about it."

"That would be nice. It's a bit lonely, being the only all-white unicorn in the forest. But what if…"

Perryn left them to it. They were the ones in the prophecy, after all. He'd done his job. He should have been jubilant, but his hands were cold. His soul felt cold. His dreams that night were filled with thundering snow and rustling wings.

THE SOUND OF THE DRAGON RETURNING TO THE valley woke them just before dawn, but it took them a while to prepare. Now Perryn stood in a small grove of trees, in the clear morning light, staring out into the valley where his mother had died. The ledge on which they had placed the cannons was easy to find. A huge snowbank overhung it like a threat. Before he'd completed his research no one had known much about avalanches; still, Perryn wondered how his father could have missed it.

"Be careful of that," he warned the others. "Don't end up fighting beneath it. The noise of the battle might well bring it down."

If this state of helpless worry was what command was like, it was no wonder his father drank. Lysander must have noticed Perryn's distress, for he turned abruptly and embraced him. Tears came to Perryn's eyes as he hugged the bard and he blinked fiercely. Lysander handed Perryn his harp.

"To keep till I get back," he said. "I'd hate to have it broken. I've already got an idea for the first verse."

Perryn hugged Prism, who shuffled to keep the suit of armor balanced on her back. It was amazing that Lysander had talked her into this. He stroked Sam, who was vibrating with excitement. His palm came away red with rust. He handed the sword to Lysander and watched them go together, down the long, steep slope into the valley—the bard, the unicorn, and the sword. *They were the stuff of legend. They were the prophecy.*

A scholar had no place beside them.

They stopped in the center of the valley.

"Come forth, foul wyrm!" The bard's challenge was a direct quote from the *Ballad of the Battle for Edam's Keep*, and it echoed off the rocks.

Perryn winced and glanced at the snowbank, but all was still.

Then the dragon appeared.

It crawled out of a crack in the cliffs, well above the valley floor, squinting in the bright sunlight. It yawned, its body gleaming like black iron. When the beast spread its wings

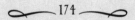

they all but covered the cliff face. Perryn hadn't dreamed it could be so big.

The dragon saw them. It paused a moment, studying them carefully. Then its laughter resounded in Perryn's mind, as dark as the depths of the earth.

The dragon launched itself, drifting easily down to stand before the companions. The spikes along its back glittered like spearheads and its bulk shadowed them like a great tree.

That was too much for Prism's newfound courage. She sank limply to the ground, the empty armor rolling and crashing around her.

The dragon laughed again. "A shiny little bauble to light the darkness of my cave." The mind-voice vibrated through Perryn's bones like an earthquake. "How long will you remain white within my darkness, I wonder? And what's this? Not a warrior, surely." It reached out and picked up Lysander as if he were a doll.

The bard lifted his arms and swung Sam with all his might.

The dragon's scream brought Perryn to his knees. He shook his head, trying to clear it, and looked fearfully at the snowbank. But there had been no real sound.

Oily blood poured from a gash in the dragon's forearm, steaming on the snow. With a roar of incredulous rage, the dragon hurled Lysander against the cliff. He fell to the snow and lay unmoving.

The dragon bent and picked up the sword, turning it curiously, like a twig in the great claws. Then the dragon grasped the sword by each end and snapped it, dropping the pieces to the ground. The creature examined its paw. Even from the hilltop where he crouched, Perryn could see the small, bleeding cut. The dragon wiped the blood on the snow, then picked up the unconscious unicorn and the bard and carried them into its cave.

Perryn ran, tripping, flailing wildly in the snow. He should have been there, should have stopped it, should have known.

He fell to his knees beside Sam, gathering the cold hilt and blade into his hands.

"Sam," he cried desperately. "What happened? What went wrong?"

"My fault, mostly." The rusty whisper was almost inaudible; Perryn could barely feel the vibration. "Didn't know it was so strong. Wanted one more fight. To die in battle, 'stead of rusting away to nothing."

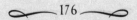

Tears rolled, unnoticed, down Perryn's cheeks. "But what about the prophecy?"

"Forget the prophecy, boy. Mardon made it up. Wanted a shot at wooing some knight's lady. Feller was a good fighter, wild for glory. Mardon thought he could send him off hunting for unicorns and dragons, but the knight didn't fall for it. Said he'd take me dragon slaying when one showed up and not before... sorry. My fault. Wanted to fight again, so bad. Didn't realize I'd bring the others down too."

"He *made it up*?"

"Well, he pro'bly didn't foresee this." Sam's chuckle was a bare whisper in Perryn's mind. Then its fading voice sobered. "You have to rescue them. Dragon'll play with them for a few days. I recognize the type. But when it gets bored... it'll kill them. You haven't much time."

"But the prophecy failed! It was fake! I can't—"

"It's not about prophecies, boy. Or magic swords, or any of that nonsense. It's about getting it done. Always is. You're going to be a king someday. Seen a lot of kings come and go. I know what makes them. What breaks them. Save your friends and kill the dragon. Or you won't be worth a cracked copper to Idris. Or to yourself. That's what it's really about . . . in the end. About you. Save them. Kill . . ."

The sword was still. Perryn let the pieces fall from his hands. He rose to his feet and stood for a moment, staring up at the cliff where the dragon had vanished.

And the prophecy failed.

12

PERRYN CROUCHED IN THE CAVE, GAZING OVER THE valley. Not even the brilliance of sunlight on snow could lighten the shadows on his heart. What could he do? Tonight, after the dragon left, he might be able to sneak into its lair and free his friends. If they still survived. But he wasn't a fighter! How could *he* challenge the dragon, when fifty of his father's best men had failed? Perhaps there was some other way—something he hadn't thought of.

With shaking hands Perryn pulled the Mirror of Idris from his pack. "Please, Mirror, is there some way...show me a way to rescue Lysander and Prism from the dragon."

Colors washed over the face of the mirror, swirling sluggishly, then the image formed. It was dusk on a bleak mountain crag. An old Norseman stood, gazing at the sky.

The leather of his shirt was painted with bright designs and stitched all over with small bones and beads—more decoration than the Norse warriors wore—and his long, gray hair streamed in the wind.

A pair of warriors stood nearby, two children beside them. The boy was weeping and the girl's face was pale and dazed, a dark bruise spreading across it. Were they . . . ? Perryn looked closely. Yes, their hands were bound. His stomach clenched with dread, even before the dragon's shadow flowed over them.

The warriors flinched when the great beast landed but the old man, the shaman, stepped forward and raised his hand.

Perryn didn't understand the Norse language, though the dragon evidently did. The shaman spoke to the dragon for a long time, gesturing frequently toward the south, where Idris lay.

Horror crept through Perryn's heart. His father had speculated that the Norsemen had sent the dragon to cripple Idris, though no one had been able to figure out how they could control the great beast. There had been rumors, whispered horrors, but Perryn hadn't really believed them. Slanders against an enemy were commonplace in any war.

But the truth lay before him now. Had the scene Perryn watched taken place in the distant past? Or worse—much worse!—did it happen every year?

The shaman stopped talking and gestured to the warriors, who dragged the children forward. The boy began to scream. The girl was struggling.

Perryn dropped the mirror and clapped his hands over his ears, closing his eyes till he was certain the image had vanished.

He felt sick, sick to his stomach, sick at heart. How could he—*worthless*, his father's voice whispered—possibly stop that?

Didn't the prince of Idris have to try?

Perhaps he could sneak into the dragon's lair, free his friends, run south. He could live in safety for years, maybe for the rest of his life. But if he ran away without confronting the dragon, without trying to save his people, it would prove that his father was right about him. Forever.

Perryn gazed over the valley where his mother had died, and the eyes behind the spectacles were no longer the eyes of a scholar. He'd already wasted part of the day and there was much to plan, and to do, before he could challenge the dragon.

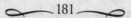

Go with your strengths.

He had to try.

PERRYN FED STICKS INTO THE SMALL FIRE WITH weary determination. He had heard the sweep of the dragon's wings passing over the cave shortly after sunset, so he felt safe in kindling this small flame. He was using King Albion's helmet as a kettle, to boil down the remaining water from the black bog. He hoped that if it became thick enough it would work as a poison instead of a sleeping potion, but he had no way to test it, and no time.

When he wasn't feeding the fire Perryn sharpened the ax. There was almost no moon, but the starlight reflected off the snow. He could see well enough.

He picked up the armor Prism had dropped and stuffed it with snow. He braced its legs with sticks he had gathered throughout the day, packing the joints so it stood in the likeness of a man, one arm upraised in challenge. He tore his spare shirt into strips and tied Sam's broken hilt into its fist. His wet gloves froze on the icy metal if he let his hands rest there too long, and the heat of his exertion fogged his spectacles.

It was easy to conceal the snare loop in the trampled

snow, to rig the snare to spring as Lysander had taught him—one of the many skills he'd acquired on this journey. Scholarship wasn't worthless, but it had its limits.

The trees here were small and stunted, but Perryn found one that he could bend without help. He feared it wouldn't last long against the dragon's strength.

When he finished, he looked up past the heavy shelf of suspended snow till he spotted the outcropping of rock he had located earlier that day. A single pine tree grew near it.

To take the old powder kegs from the cave up to the rim of the valley, he had to circle around its edge. One keg was slung against his chest, the other on his back. He carried the ax, the shovel, and the third torch in his hands. He had to tear up his cloak to make the slings, but even so, he was sweating when he reached the place on the cliff top that he had marked from below.

Perryn dropped his gear and sank down, his chest heaving. The stars that had risen at sunset had almost crossed the sky—not much time till dawn. The dragon might return sooner than that, and he dared not rest too long in the cold lest his muscles stiffen.

Perryn picked up the shovel and began to dig.

THE SKY WAS BRIGHTENING, AND IF HE DUG ANY
deeper he wouldn't be able to climb out of the hole.

Perryn laid one barrel in the bottom of the hole and
split the lid of the other with the ax. He carefully placed
that barrel upright, digging powder out of the split with
his fingers to cover the lid. He had long since abandoned
his soaked gloves, and his hands were freezing.

He heard the windy rush of dragon wings.

Perryn bounded out of the hole. He couldn't see the
valley floor from where he stood, so he snatched up the torch
and the ax and scrambled up the rocky outcrop.

Crouching in the shadow of the pine tree, Perryn looked
down. The dragon gazed at the snow knight, standing just
outside the reach of Perryn's snare. Perryn fumbled in his
belt pouch for flint and steel and bent to kindle the torch.
His hands were steady, not shaking at all—which was odd,
for he'd never been more frightened in his life.

"So, a single challenger today. With no weapon. But
you don't smell like a mage." The dragon's voice was
softer than before, but even at this distance every word
rang clear in Perryn's mind. It sniffed again. "In fact, you

don't smell much like a man." The dragon stepped toward the unmoving knight.

Flame crackled and Perryn's torch began to burn.

"What manner of foolish creature are you?" It took another step. Perryn held his breath. The small tree sprang upright and the snare loop flew, off center, catching one of the dragon's wings.

The dragon jumped. Its head swung toward the snow knight, and flame burst from its mouth, consuming the armor of the twenty-seventh warrior-king of Idris. The dragon sniffed at the pile of collapsed metal, laughed, and began to untangle the rope from the most fragile part of its great frame.

Perryn dropped the torch into the hole and ducked. The blast shook the rock, and he clutched at the tree. Snow rained down on top of him.

In the silence that followed, the mountains seemed to breathe.

The dragon stopped pulling at the rope and stared upward. A rumble started and grew louder. Almost in slow motion, the huge bank of snow began to fall.

Suddenly, the dragon understood. It yanked violently on

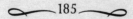

the rope, but the young tree bent and absorbed the strain.

The snow crashed down the mountainside, gathering speed as it fell. The thunder of the avalanche consumed the dragon's roar.

Another stream of fire shot from the dragon's mouth. The tree burst into flame, and the rope snapped, but it was too late. Billowing with white spray, the avalanche engulfed the great beast like a tidal wave, swept it down the valley, and covered it.

The rumbling died. No more snow fell. Perryn heard nothing. He wasn't sure if there was nothing to hear, or if the noise had deafened him. Then he sat up, and the scrape of his boots against the rock was startlingly loud. He let go of the tree. He had gripped the rough bark so hard his palms were bleeding. There was no trace of the dragon. More than anything else, Perryn wanted to flee the valley, to grab Prism and Lysander and just go.

But discovering facts wasn't a scholar's only job—he also faced the truth.

People buried near the surface had dug their way out of avalanches, and the dragon was stronger than any man. The dragon thrived on cold.

Perryn looked carefully over the valley, noting the place the dragon had gone under as well as he could. Then he picked up the ax and started down.

PERRYN STOOD ON THE SLIPPERY, HARD-PACKED snow and waited, ax in hand.

He had found a piece of his cloak at the top of the cliff and wrapped it around himself, but the rest of it was gone. He shivered convulsively, but he was barely aware of the cold.

Malthin wrote that the only way to fight a magical creature was with magic. But Bocaccus, in *The Anatomy of All Creatures*, had proved that severing its spine would kill any living thing. Perryn watched the snowfield and wondered where the dragon would emerge. And when. He prayed it would be never, but he couldn't leave until he was certain.

He'd coated the ax head with the condensed black bog water. That might be magic. Or it might not even be poisonous. Perryn could experiment with it someday, if he survived. He wondered if Prism and Lysander were all right. He didn't dare to wonder if they were still alive.

The snow to his left stirred. Or was it a trick of the eyes? Slipping and sliding, Perryn hurried over to the spot. His heart pounded.

Nothing. A trick.

Then the snow heaved violently, and the dragon's head burst through. Perryn was standing to its side. The beast's neck stretched upward, and Perryn swung the ax at its exposed throat.

A small gash appeared. The dragon turned and saw Perryn, who tried to jump away and slipped. The dragon's mighty head smashed him down, into the snow, the ax flying from Perryn's hand. The small spikes along its jaw tore into Perryn's leg, and he cried out.

The dragon's head lifted. As it struggled to free its body, Perryn rolled and snatched up the ax. In a slithering, scrambling crawl, he managed to get behind the dragon. As the back of its neck rose above the snow, he saw the ridge of sharp spikes that ran along it, marking the position of the spine. Perryn drew a shaking breath and swung the ax again.

It was like striking a column of iron. The blow jarred his arms to the shoulders, but another cut appeared, oozing dark blood.

"I will roast your bones," the dragon's voice reverberated in Perryn's thoughts. It twisted its head to breathe fire, but Perryn stepped right up behind its neck, and the flame shot off to one side.

He swung the ax again.

The dragon's head snapped back, trying to crush him, and the spikes on its spine tore open Perryn's shoulder. He fell to his knees. The dragon's head swung again, but it couldn't bend its neck far enough to reach him. From his knees, Perryn swung the ax again, and again.

"I will destroy you!" the dragon roared. Perryn's brain went numb under the blast, but his hands and body found the familiar rhythm, and he worked steadily, chopping through the writhing spine.

The dragon roared again, but Perryn could no longer distinguish words.

Blood burst out as he severed a vein, splattering his spectacles and obscuring his vision. It stung as it seeped into the wound in his shoulder, but Perryn chopped on without pause.

A fragment of music drifted through his mind, blending with the rhythm of the ax, but he couldn't place it. His

world had narrowed in a woodcutter's concentration. Nothing existed but the ax and the target.

With a soft crack, the dragon's spine broke. Perryn lowered the ax. He was standing, though he didn't remember rising to his feet. The dragon lay still, its head rolled awkwardly to one side.

Perryn's shoulder burned as if flames consumed it. His blood burned. The dragon's blood was everywhere. *Dragon's wrath*. It would be this dragon's final anger.

Perryn fell, but he didn't hit the ground. Strong arms caught him. He heard Lysander's voice, though he didn't understand what the bard said. The last thing he saw, before his sight failed, was Prism, walking steadily toward him through the filthy, blood-soaked snow.

HE WAS LYING AGAINST PRISM WHEN HE CAME TO. They had carried him out of the valley to the shelter of the cave and lit a fire, even though it was broad day.

"Because once Prism took care of the fever, you were freezing," the bard explained.

"You must be cold yourself." Perryn was wrapped in the bard's cloak.

"I'm fine," said Lysander. "Better than fine, now I'm out of that stinking hole."

Perryn understood. His torn calf and shoulder throbbed, and every muscle in his body ached, but he felt wonderful. He'd managed to tell them what happened to Sam, and what the sword had said.

"What happened to you?" Perryn asked.

"We woke up in a cage," said the bard. "The dragon must have used it to store dinner. Evidently, it preferred the freshest meat."

"The freshest meat?"

"Nothing fresher than live." The bard's voice was light, but his expression wasn't.

"The cage was filthy," Prism added primly.

"It was obviously designed to hold cattle or deer," the bard continued. "Climbing out was no problem once the dragon left. Before that," he shivered, "it was watching us."

"It wanted to eat me," said Prism indignantly. "But Lysander stopped it."

"Not stopped," said the bard. "Only delayed. I talked, sang, told jokes—"

"It had a horrible sense of humor," said Prism.

"I've never had a tougher audience," Lysander admitted. "Or one I was happier to see leave. After I escaped I had to find a way to free Prism. It would have been easy, if it hadn't been so blasted dark. I had to do everything by touch, and then it took the rest of the night to grope our way out of the cave. We reached the entrance just as the dragon poked its head out of the snow. Then we had to get down the cliff without breaking our necks. Fortunately, Prism got to you in time."

"So you saved Prism, and Prism saved me." Perryn reached out and stroked the unicorn's flank. Three gray dapples bloomed there. "I'm sorry."

"I don't know if I am," said Prism. "I'll get more respect around the forest now. Perhaps there's something to be said for fulfilling your destiny. Not too quickly, of course."

Perryn smiled. "Will you go south now?" he asked the bard.

Lysander shrugged. "No reason to. Now that the dragon's dead, your father's men will be able to hold back the Norsemen. Though it will be warmer in the south. And richer." He grinned at Perryn and then sobered. "We

heard the avalanche. I see the powder is gone so I can guess most of it, and you can tell me the rest later. But what will you do now? Your father will have to respect you, after this."

"Maybe. I'm not sure my father has enough strength to change, not anymore." The knowledge still hurt, deep inside. *But a scholar faced the truth.* "I have to go home and tell him what happened, and about Cedric, but then I'm going south. I'm going to study in the universities."

The magic of men might be fading from the world, but the magic the gods had wrought was still strong. The north held other dragons, and sooner or later the Norsemen would find a way to bind one to their service. There had to be a way to defeat them, with or without magic. Some answer a scholar could find.

Lysander whistled. "Your father won't like that. Warrior or not, you're still going to be the forty-fifth king of Idris."

"I know," said Perryn. "And I want to be." How strange to feel so certain of it. Worthy of it. "But it will be on my terms," he added. "Not my father's."

"I see," said the bard softly.

"I could never have done it without you," Perryn told them. "Both of you. And Sam." His throat tightened with grief and love.

"So, in a way," said Prism, "the prophecy came true. Didn't it?"

Lysander snorted.

Perryn smiled.

And thus it is recorded that in
later years, when Perryndon,
the first of the great scholar-kings
of Idris, was asked if he believed in
the power of prophecy,
he simply smiled and said nothing.

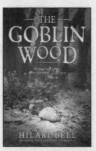

DATE DUE

FEB 2 5 '08		
MAR 2 5 '08		
MAY 0 7 '08		
NOV 0 3 '08		
DEC 0 8 '08		
APR 0 3 '09		
APR 1 7 '09		
MAY 1 1 '09		
MAY 1 0 '70		
JAN 1 7 '12		